KT-497-592

THE TOMB IN TURKEY

THE TOMB IN TURKEY

A *Fethering Mystery*

Simon Brett

CRÈME de la CRIME

This first world edition published 2014
in Great Britain and 2015 in the USA by
Crème de la Crime, an imprint of
SEVERN HOUSE PUBLISHERS LTD of
19 Cedar Road, Sutton, Surrey, England, SM2 5DA.
Trade paperback edition first published
in Great Britain and the USA 2015 by
SEVERN HOUSE PUBLISHERS LTD.

Copyright © 2014 by Simon Brett.

All rights reserved.
The moral right of the author has been asserted.

British Library Cataloguing in Publication Data

Brett, Simon author.
  The Tomb in Turkey. – (A Fethering mystery)
  1. Seddon, Carole (Fictitious character)–Fiction. 2. Jude
  (Fictitious character: Brett)–Fiction. 3. Women private
  investigators–England–Fiction. 4. Murder–
  Investigation–Turkey–Fiction. 5. Tombs–Turkey–
  Fiction. 6. Detective and mystery stories.
  I. Title II. Series
  823.9'2-dc23

ISBN-13: 978-1-78029-069-0 (cased)
ISBN-13: 978-1-78029-551-0 (trade paper)
ISBN-13: 978-1-78010-606-9 (e-book)

Except where actual historical events and characters are being
described for the storyline of this novel, all situations in this
publication are fictitious and any resemblance to living persons
is purely coincidental.

All Severn House titles are printed on acid-free paper.

Severn House Publishers support the Forest Stewardship Council™ [FSC™],
the leading international forest certification organisation. All our titles that
are printed on FSC certified paper carry the FSC logo.

Typeset by Palimpsest Book Production Ltd.,
Falkirk, Stirlingshire, Scotland.
Printed and bound in Great Britain by
TJ International, Padstow, Cornwall.

To Jean,
with many thanks for keeping the
Brett Family Machine
running over the years

And with thanks to Recep and Clare
for their expertise on scuba diving

ABERDEENSHIRE LIBRARIES	
3152941	
Bertrams	14/11/2014
MYS	£19.99

ONE

'Go on holiday?' Carole Seddon echoed in disbelief. 'Why?'

She was totally amazed by her neighbour Jude's suggestion. Holidays while she still had a full-time job at the Home Office had made some kind of sense. Carole had never enjoyed them much, either when she was married to David and they had family holidays with their son Stephen, or later after the divorce, but she could see the point of them then. Now, retired to the south-coast village of Fethering, itself a summer destination for day-trippers, why would she need a holiday?

'Well, we could both do with a break,' Jude said, the ghost of a smile lurking around her full lips.

'A break from what?' asked Carole testily.

'Well, I know you think what I do is on the barmier side of black magic, but in fact being a healer brings its own stresses. It takes a lot out of me. I've had a continuous stream of clients in the past few months, and I am . . . not to put too fine a point on it . . . knackered.'

'Maybe,' said Carole, 'but what about me? What would I be taking a break *from*?'

It was one of those rare moments when Carole Seddon was almost playing for sympathy. Though she always claimed when asked to be 'busy, busy, busy', there was an emptiness at her core. Apart from keeping her house High Tor at a level of cleanliness that would not have shamed an Intensive Care Unit, doing *The Times* crossword, and taking her Labrador Gulliver for long walks on Fethering Beach, there wasn't a lot in her life. There were, of course, Stephen, his wife Gaby and Carole's adored granddaughter Lily, but though they were only in Fulham, she didn't see that much of them.

The fact was that Carole Seddon, after a good few years of it, still hadn't properly adjusted to retirement. The Calvinist streak in her make-up made her feel that she should always be working. And beneath a pile of other resentments was the irksome memory that she had been retired early from the Home Office, and not at a time of her choosing. In her mind, for someone like her to contemplate taking a holiday would be the height of self-indulgence.

'Why not,' asked Jude, 'take a holiday just for the hell of it?'

'I don't,' replied Carole primly, 'do anything just for the hell of it.'

Which was exactly the answer Jude could have predicted. With a grin she went on, 'Well, I need a holiday.'

'But you always seem to be going off for odd weekends for healing conventions, mind and body conferences, holistic workshops, reiki retreats . . .' With the mention of each event, Carole had more difficulty in keeping the scepticism out of her voice.

'What you don't realize is that those things are part of my job—'

'Huh.'

'—and they're actually quite hard work. It's tiring, you know, networking, listening to lectures, catching up with the latest trends . . .'

But that only got another, 'Huh.'

'Anyway, given the offer of a free holiday, I'm going to take it.'

One word caught Carole's attention. 'Free?'

'Well, free bar the flights. Free once we – or I – get there.'

Carole Seddon's face took on the expression of a hanging judge. 'Are you caught up in some *timeshare scam*, Jude?' The words were italicized in best *Daily Mail* style.

'No, of course I'm not! I just have a friend who owns a villa, and he's offered me the use of it for a week or two.'

'Free?'

'Yes, I said free.'

'Why?'

'Why what?'

'Why would he offer you the use of his villa free?'

'Because he's a friend.'

'He's not a friend of mine.'

'No. You haven't met him.'

'Then why would he offer me a free week or two in his villa?' The level of suspicion in Carole's tone was mounting.

Jude's tone, by contrast, was as near as it ever got to exasperated (which wasn't very near). 'He's not offering *you* anything.'

'Oh.' Slightly miffed now.

'He's offered me the villa and, assuming that I don't want to spend a fortnight on my own in foreign climes, he said I could invite a friend.'

'Oh.' Mollified.

'Or a group of friends.'

'Oh.' Less mollified. The idea of finding herself on holiday with a bunch of people she didn't know was one of Carole's worst nightmares. The thought of having breakfast with them, making conversation, joining in with enforced jollity . . . it didn't bear thinking of.

'And so I thought I'd ask you first if you wanted to come.'

Carole remembered her manners. 'Well, that's very kind of you.'

'But since you apparently don't, I'll—'

'Ah, now I didn't say that.'

'You did as near as dammit. You said, "Why?" . . . in a way that implied you'd never heard a worse idea.'

'Well, that may be how it came across, but it wasn't quite how I meant it.'

'Oh?'

'I mean I'd like to know a bit more about the circumstances, about the gentleman who's made you this generous offer.'

'All right,' said Jude. 'His name's Barney Willingdon. He's a property developer, been very successful.'

'Then why's he offering the villa to you? You don't normally deal with property developers, do you?' Carole Seddon fixed her pale-blue eyes on her neighbour's brown ones. 'Is he someone . . . from your past?'

Jude knew exactly what the question meant. Her sex life had been quite varied over the years – though not as varied and busy as Carole always seemed to think it had been. She was being asked whether Barney Willingdon had ever been one of her lovers.

'It's nothing like that,' she said, carefully avoiding a direct answer. 'I've done some healing work with his wife, Henry.'

'Henry?'

'Short for Henrietta.'

'Ah. What was wrong with her?'

'Now you know I can't tell you that, Carole.'

This prompted a sniff. Carole couldn't really see why the rules of client confidentiality should apply to healers, who were really only one generation away from witch doctors.

Jude went on, 'Barney's made the offer of the villa by way of a thank you.'

'Oh, I see.' Carole took a moment to think about the situation. One thing she had avoided all her life – with an almost paranoid terror – was being 'beholden' to anyone. Her parents had never liked being 'beholden'. Nothing should be taken if something else was not offered by way of recompense. This rule had applied to all their dealings – financial, social and emotional – and it was a habit of thought that Carole found hard to break.

'So . . .' she began cautiously, 'I'd be sort of riding on the back of the goodwill that Barney feels towards you?'

'Oh, for heaven's sake, Carole, you do make things complicated.'

'No, I don't. I just like to know where I stand. And if I were contemplating going on a free holiday I'd want to know what—'

'Ah, so you are contemplating doing it?'

'I didn't say that I was.'

'But you might be.'

'Well . . .'

'Come on, Carole, it'd be fun.'

'"Fun"?' Carole contemplated the unfamiliar concept.

'Yes. And we know each other well enough not to get on each other's nerves.' (Though Jude wondered, given the way Carole was currently behaving, how true that assertion was.)

'Hm. And when were you thinking of this holiday happening? Because I told you Gaby is pregnant again—'

'Many times.'

'—and I wouldn't want to be abroad when—'

'The baby is due at the end of October, Carole. There is plenty of time.'

'When were you thinking of going, then?'

'June.'

'But that's less than a month away.'

'The sooner the better, so far as I'm concerned. And Barney says the villa's booked solid for July and August, as you would expect.'

'Does he go out there himself?'

'Yes, he spends a lot of time out there, either in that one or one of the others.'

'"One of the others"?'

'Barney owns a lot of villas.'

'Oh, really?' Carole suspected yet another downside. 'What, in blocks . . .? You mean crammed on top of each other like battery chickens?'

'No,' said Jude patiently. 'They're all high-spec luxury villas, set in their own grounds, with their own swimming pools. It's just that Barney has built quite a lot of them. I told you he's a property developer. He's a major operator.'

'Really?' said Carole dubiously. The expression 'property developer' was not one that raised her confidence. But before she could express her doubts, a vital question came into her mind, a question that she should really have asked a lot earlier.

'One thing, Jude . . . You haven't actually said what country Barney's villas are in.'

'Turkey.'

'Turkey?' echoed Carole, as only Carole could.

It was presumably the sales of Barney Willingdon's properties abroad that enabled him to live in such an opulent property in England. Chantry House was a genuinely Tudor pile, with extensive grounds, set in a wooded area just north of Petworth. It was a sunny early evening in May as Carole's Renault drew up on the immaculately raked gravel drive. Both women were impressed by the scale of the house and its high level of maintenance. No expense had been spared anywhere. Also on the gravel stood a substantial Rolls-Royce. It had a 'BW' personalized number plate, which Carole thought was rather vulgar. But she didn't make any comment.

What she did say, though, was, 'Now, remember, Jude, I haven't committed myself to anything.'

'I will remember,' Jude asserted solemnly.

'I just want to meet Barney and hear more about this villa of his. I still haven't said I'm going to go there.'

Jude nodded, again solemnly. Carole's reaction was so characteristic, but Jude was beginning to wonder whether the whole holiday project was going to be more trouble than it was worth. If she'd asked her reflexologist friend Jools to join her for a fortnight in Turkey, the reaction would have been instantaneous, without any fuss. In fact, she had asked Jools, but her friend was at a delicate stage of a new relationship with a man she'd met at a self-awareness workshop and couldn't risk being away from England. (Jude devoutly reminded herself that the one thing she must never do was to let Carole know she hadn't been first choice for the holiday offer. That knowledge could prompt all kinds of recrimination and sniffiness.)

'Fine,' Jude said. 'I will tell Barney that you *may* be coming with me.'

'You don't think he'll think that's rude . . . you know, as if I were, kind of, looking his gift horse in the mouth?'

'And what are you doing . . . if you're not looking his gift horse in the mouth?'

'Well, I . . .'

'It'll be fine, Carole. Just relax.'

'That's easy for you to say.'

TWO

'**A**nd there's a ghost town,' said Barney Willingdon.

'A ghost town?' echoed Carole.

'Yes. End of the village. Some quirk of history. I don't know all the details, but I think the people who lived there used to be Greeks.'

'Anatolians,' his wife Henry corrected him. She was a thin, flimsy-looking woman with ash-blonde hair. Maybe in her forties, could have been fifties. She wore black designer jeans and a white blouse with a design of violets on it. Her public-school vowels contrasted strongly with her husband's local Sussex accent.

'Yeah, whatever. Anyway, they was Christians in a Muslim country, and there was a kind of population exchange with some Greek Muslims coming back to Turkey and these people going back to wherever they—'

'Anatolia,' said Henry.

'Right. This was in the 1920s.'

'Nineteen twenty-three.'

'Sure, Henry. So, anyway, all these Gr— Anatolians just upped sticks and moved out, and the town's still there, all set on this hillside, virtually as they left it. A few of the houses have been restored – very few – but most of them have been empty all that time. Windows gone, roofs fallen in, but most of the stone walls are still standing.'

'Sounds like a good place to wander round,' said Jude.

'You'd love it, darling. Fabulous place, Kayaköy.'

'That's the name of the village?'

'Right, Carole. I got half a dozen villas out there, but the one'd be perfect for you two is called Morning Glory. Set up a bit on the hills, lovely view over the valley . . . infinity pool, all mod cons. You'd love it, Jude.'

'Sounds great.'

'But how would one deal with, sort of . . . everyday things?'

'Sorry, Carole? Wodja mean?'

'Well, neither of us speaks any Turkish or—'

'No worries. Most of the locals speak English. Certainly all the ones involved in the tourist business, and in Kayaköy most of them are.'

This prompted a new suspicion in Carole. 'So is it very touristy?'

'No, that's the beauty of the place. Near some very touristy places . . . Ölüdeniz, Hisarönü . . . but Kayaköy itself is remarkably unspoilt.'

'It does sound blissful,' said Jude.

They were in the Willingdons' sitting room, drinking an absolutely delicious New Zealand Sauvignon Blanc, whose bottle lolled in an ice bucket with another unopened by its side. The evening was warm enough for the French windows to be open, showing perfect lawns rolling down to the edge of the woodland. The room's interior was beautifully designed with what Carole thought was a surprising degree of taste. The inherent prejudices which the words 'property developer' brought to her mind included lots of onyx and swirly carpets. And when they'd been greeted at the door by Barney Willingdon he had reinforced that expectation. A large man, full of restless energy, he had longish hair and a trim beard beginning to give way to grey. He wore a tailored leather jacket above designer jeans, and his body seemed to taper down to surprisingly small loafers with leather tassels on them. His size and rough vowels were at odds with the elegance of his surroundings. Carole suspected that Henry Willingdon had had more input into the decor of Chantry House than her husband.

Jude, too, was making observations about the environment in which they found themselves, but hers were more personal. And, of course, she knew a little more than Carole about the Willingdons from the healing sessions she had given to Henry. She knew that theirs was a second marriage for Barney and that he was some twelve years older than his new wife. The lack of photographs in the sitting room reinforced Jude's impression that both marriages had been childless. And the peremptory way in which she had corrected her husband suggested that, in spite of her pale wispiness, Henry was at least an equal partner in the relationship. And possibly even the dominant one.

'Anyway,' said Barney, 'if you have any problems out at Morning Glory, I have an extensive network of people on the ground out there who can sort everything. Plumbing, electrics, problems with the pool or the car, leaking roof . . . there's a list of phone numbers in the villa that will instantly summon up the best in the business. I've worked out there so much, I know everyone.'

'Or their cousin,' said Henry.

'Yes.' Her husband grinned. 'They're all cousins out there.

Someone can't fix something – no worries, he'll have a cousin
who can. They're a really friendly lot.'

Henry seemed about to say something which might have
qualified this statement, but a look from Barney stopped her.

'And they will be able to tell us about the best places to go
out for the odd day?' asked Jude. 'Best beaches, archaeological
sites, what-have-you . . .?'

'We can get that information from guidebooks,' said Carole,
forgetting that she hadn't yet committed herself to going to
Kayaköy. 'Or online.'

'Sure,' said Barney, 'but much better if you get it from
people who're based there. They really know the area. Anyway,
the person you want to talk to about that stuff is an
Englishwoman called Nita Davies. She's a great friend of
ours.'

'A great friend of *yours*,' Henry interposed pointedly.

'Whatever.' Barney went on: 'Nita's married to a Turk, guy
called Erkan. But in fact she still uses her maiden name profes-
sionally . . . which is just as well because her married surname
is totally unpronounceable. So she's still Nita Davies. Actually,
he might be useful to you, Erkan. He runs a diving school, so
if you were to fancy a bit of the old scuba . . .?'

'I don't think I probably will,' said Jude.

'I'm certain that I won't,' said Carole.

'Up to you. Anyway, Nita still works as a rep for one of
the travel companies. Forget which one, she keeps changing
jobs. But she knows the area inside out.'

'Does she act as a rep for your villa company?' asked Carole.

'No, I've got a manager out there who looks after all the
villas. And since all the booking's done online these days,
we don't need an office here in the UK. So, like I say, you'll
have plenty of English speakers in Kayaköy to look after you.
And you'll have the use of a car, obviously.'

'Really?'

'Sure thing, Jude. Henry and I're out in Kayaköy so often
we—'

'*You're* out in Kayaköy so often,' his wife once again
interposed.

'Yeah. So we've got a car out there permanently. Fiat it is.'

'But what about insurance?' It was Carole who asked the question. Jude would never have thought of it.

'All sorted. I just need to let them know your details and you can drive wherever you want.'

'That's great,' said Jude.

'So it's really just a matter of the dates.' Barney Willingdon reached into the pocket of his leather jacket and produced a state-of-the-art smartphone. 'As I said, it'll have to be before the beginning of July.' He reached the diary. 'So when do you fancy? And for how long?'

This wasn't something the two women had discussed. Carole had been so tentative about the whole project that they hadn't got down to such basic details. So Jude gave the dates that would be ideal for her. Two weeks, and leaving in twelve days' time, assuming she could arrange the flights.

'Should be all right this early in the season,' said Barney. 'And if you do have any problems, I'll put you in touch with Nita. She's got contacts with the airlines. She can fix anything.'

'Oh yes,' Henry agreed without great warmth. 'She's a real Mrs Fix-It, our Nita.'

Barney flashed a look of exasperation at his wife before moving on. 'Actually, you may well see us out there too.'

'Oh, you'll be in Kayaköy?' asked Jude.

'Maybe. There's another couple of villas I'm building outside Ölüdeniz, and the contractors there could do with a kick up the arse, so yes, we may be there.'

'But it's not very likely,' said Henry. 'We haven't firmed up our plans yet. Not for both of us going, anyway.'

Barney Willingdon's expression suggested that this was a subject they'd argued about before. And would argue about again when they were on their own. 'Look,' he said to his guests, 'you check out the flights and get back to me. As I say, anytime you like before the beginning of July.'

'Well, it's very generous of you, Barney,' said Jude. 'Are you sure I can't contribute something towards—?'

He raised both hands to stop her in mid-flow. 'Absolutely not. I won't hear of it. The villa's there, it's not costing me anything for you to use it. And after everything you've done for Henry . . .'

What did she do for Henry? Carole wondered. She wondered also about the chances of Jude ever telling her. She wasn't optimistic. Her neighbour could sometimes be very old-fashioned about client confidentiality . . . just as if she were a proper doctor.

As the Renault drove away from Chantry House, Jude, buoyed up by the interest Carole had shown in the practical details of the villa, asked, 'Will those dates be all right for you?'

'Oh,' said Carole rather sniffily, 'I haven't decided whether I'm going to come yet.'

THREE

'So how's Gaby?'
'Pretty good, actually. The morning sickness seems to have stopped, and she's entering the blooming phase of pregnancy.'

'Oh.' When she'd been expecting the baby who became the man at the other end of the phone, Carole hadn't had a 'blooming' phase – at least, not that she could recollect. But then she hadn't much liked any aspect of carrying Stephen. 'And has Lily taken on board that she's going to have a new brother or sister?'

'Well, we've told her enough times, but whether she's taken it on board is another matter. Her main preoccupation seems to be playing with princess dolls.'

'Very right and proper for a child of her age,' said the fond grandmother (who was far from 'right on' when it came to gender politics). 'Stephen . . .'

'Yes, Mother?'

Carole still wished her son would relax enough to call her 'Mummy'. Or even 'Mum', though that, of course, was rather vulgar. 'I wondered how you'd react if I were to go away for a while . . .?'

'Go away? Where to?'

'I've been offered a chance of a week or a fortnight's holiday in Turkey.'

'Well, that sounds wonderful. Who're you going with?'

'If I go, it'll be with Jude. You know Jude?'

'Yes, of course. Your neighbour, the hippy-dippy healer. Well, it sounds a jolly good idea to me.'

'But you're sure you won't need me around?' The question was almost plaintive.

'What for?' The question wasn't the most tactful that Stephen Seddon had ever posed.

'Well, you know, if Gaby needs help with Lily like she did earlier in the pregnancy, or if she—'

'No, no, Gaby's as fit as a fiddle now. No problems with Lily. And if there are any, Gaby's got a network of local friends who can help out. No, you go to Turkey. Have a great time. When are you off?'

'Oh, I haven't definitely decided I'm going yet.'

When she finished the phone call, Carole felt a little bereft. She didn't realize the delight that grown-up children who have their own children feel when a parent makes their own holiday arrangements. It removes both a level of anxiety and a level of guilt. It's another year that they don't have the feeling they should be including the grandparent in their own holiday plans.

'I'm really not sure, Jude.'

'Well, I'm afraid I need a decision pretty quickly. The flights need booking.'

'Yes, I can see that. It's just that . . . well, we've never been on holiday together, have we?'

'No, but we've done lots of other things together, so it's no big deal. And from the sound of the villa, it's big enough for us not to live in each other's pockets. Some days we can do stuff together, other days we can be on our own.'

'Yes . . .'

The monosyllable was so unconvinced that Jude asked, 'What're you really worried about?'

'Oh, I'm not worried,' Carole lied. (She was always worried.) 'It's just it's a very long time since I've been on a holiday . . . and I've never been on this kind of Mediterranean holiday . . . and, well, you say we could do "stuff" together. What kind of stuff?'

'Whatever we wanted to do.'

'So what might you want to do?'

'On holiday?'

'Yes.'

'You're asking me what my idea of a holiday is?'

'I suppose I am.'

'Well, my idea – or my ideal – would be lolling about by the pool on a lounger, reading some kind of trashy novel, taking the occasional splash in the pool, going out for lots of nice meals, sitting out after dark with a nice drink . . . That'd do me.'

'Hm. That sounds very . . . *laid-back*.' Carole had difficulty speaking the alien expression.

'Well, that's what I need. For the first few days, anyway. I may be up for the odd excursion later into the holiday.'

'Hm.'

'Why, Carole? What's your idea of a holiday?'

'I don't really know,' she was forced to admit.

'Look, it doesn't matter. Going on holiday isn't like taking an exam. Nobody has any expectations of what you do. It's just an opportunity to *relax*.'

Carole's expression suggested she found this concept as alien as being 'laid-back'.

There was a silence. They were drinking coffee in the amiable chaos of Jude's sitting room. The May mini heatwave was continuing, but there was enough breeze to set the bamboo wind-chimes hanging at the windows tinkling. When she had first entered Woodside Cottage, Carole had found the sound irritating, yet another example of her neighbour's New Age flakiness. Now she found the chimes rather soothing.

'Sorry to nag,' said Jude, 'but I'm afraid I do need a decision from you.'

'Of course, yes. I can see that.'

'Well . . .?'

'It's difficult . . .' Carole began.

'It is not at all difficult. Or if there is a difficulty it can only be a practical one. Have you got other commitments you can't postpone for the time we're proposing to be away? Is it that you can't afford it?'

'Good heavens no,' replied Carole, rather affronted. Her money management was very precise; she even managed to save quite a substantial amount of her generous Home Office pension. She would never even contemplate doing something she couldn't afford and was appalled that Jude thought she might.

'Well then, I must have a decision from you. I need to book the flights.'

'And are you thinking of one week or two?'

'Oh, it has to be two weeks. Go for one week, you spend the first half untwitching and the second half twitching up again.'

'I think I could only manage a week,' said Carole before hastily adding: 'That is, if I were to go.'

'Well, that'd be fine. You could come back at the end of the first week, and I could stay on for another.'

'On your own?'

'Yes, of course on my own.'

'But would you feel safe?'

'I would feel perfectly safe. It's Turkey we're talking about, not Syria.'

'But Turkey's a Muslim country . . .'

'Yes.'

'And Muslims aren't very friendly towards women.'

'Carole, where on earth did you get that from?'

'I read the papers. I watch television.'

Jude always found it strange that for someone whose daily paper was *The Times*, Carole could sometimes be so *Daily Mail* in her views. 'Turkey,' said Jude patiently, 'is an extremely civilized country. I'd feel safer there than I would in Brighton.'

'Hm,' said Carole. 'Have you checked out availability of flights?'

'No, I haven't,' said Jude, in a tone which was as near as she ever got to exasperation. 'Because I don't know whether I'm booking one flight or two, do I?'

'I've done some research.'

'On flights?'

'Yes. Online, of course,' said Carole. 'You'd be amazed the number of offers there are . . . if you shop around.'

Jude, a creature of impulse to whom the concept of 'shopping around' was anathema, just said, 'And?'

'Well, there are quite a lot of flights to Dalaman this time of year . . .'

'Good. I thought there would be.'

'. . . but a lot of them go from Heathrow or Luton or Stansted, which is rather out of the way for us.'

'We really need to fly from Gatwick.'

'That's what I thought. Well, there is availability.'

'For the dates we want?'

'Yes. I've checked out both the one week and two week options.'

'Where did you check them out?'

'On a price comparison website.'

'Oh.' Jude would never have bothered to do that. She'd have just gone for the first option that presented itself. She wasn't very good at the minutiae of budgeting. She understood the meaning of the word 'budget', but not its practical application.

'There's quite a big difference between the most expensive and the cheapest.'

'Really?'

'Over a hundred pounds.'

'Wow.'

'But I've managed to get a very good deal.' And Carole told Jude the price. Which was a very good deal indeed.

'And we can get that deal on the dates we want?'

'Yes, there is availability. And I've put a hold on the flights through an agent.'

'For the one week or the two?'

'Both. I have to give the agent confirmation by the end of tomorrow.'

'Oh, that's brilliant, Carole. I'm rubbish at doing stuff like that. Thank you so much.'

'Don't worry. I quite enjoy doing "stuff like that".'

'And I also meant to say thank you for deciding that you are joining me in Turkey.'

'Oh, I haven't decided whether I'm going to come yet,' said Carole.

'On your own then?' asked Ted Crisp. 'No Carole?'

It was half-past five. Jude had felt like a change of scene, and the Crown and Anchor, Fethering's only pub, fitted the bill perfectly.

'No,' she replied, 'and it's actually quite a relief. Carole is being at her most Carole at the moment, if you know what I mean.'

'I certainly do,' said the landlord. He was a large, scruffy man with matted beard and hair. It was warm enough for him to be wearing his summer uniform of faded blue T-shirt and jeans (as opposed to his winter uniform of faded blue sweatshirt and jeans). 'Large Chilean Chardonnay, is it?' he asked, reaching to the fridge for the bottle.

'Do you know, I think I'll have something different.'

'Blimey O'Reilly,' said Ted. 'What's up? The Pope's a Catholic, bears, er, do their business in the woods, and Carole and Jude always drink Chilean Chardonnay. It's one of the immutable rules of life.'

'Maybe, but it's just that I had some New Zealand Sauvignon Blanc a couple of days ago and it was really nice. So I thought I might have a change.'

'Well, that's not a bad call, Jude. I love the old New Zealand whites. Particularly the Marlborough Sauvignons.' He produced the relevant bottle from the fridge. 'This one's a beauty. Crisp as a new apple. Still a large one, is it?'

Jude nodded.

'And do you think Lady Muck from High Tor will change from the Chilean Chardonnay too?'

'I doubt it. I can't see her wanting to do anything I do.'

'What's this then? Rifts in the lute? Less than perfect harmony between neighbours?'

'Oh, it's just, as I said, Carole being Carole.' And Jude gave Ted a precis of Carole's recent dithering over the Turkish holiday.

'If she's behaving like that, I'd have thought you'd be well shot of her. When Carole gets grumpy . . .' He didn't finish the sentence, but Jude picked up the reference. Incongruous though it might seem, Ted Crisp and Carole Seddon had at one point had a brief affair. And it was no doubt during that that he had experienced Carole getting grumpy. 'Can't you just go on your own? Or isn't there one of your many lovers around who . . .?'

'I don't have many lovers, Ted.'

'According to Carole you do.'

'She just exaggerates. For someone who claims to have no imagination, she's extremely inventive when it comes to her view of my love life. She thinks every man I speak to must have been one of my lovers at some point.'

'Isn't that rather flattering?'

'I'm not sure that it is, actually, no. Anyway, there are other friends I could ask – ones I don't actually go to bed with – but I can't do that until I get a definite yea or nay from Carole.'

'Why's she messing you around like this?'

'It's just her nature. It's how she is. Before she does anything she has to go through great rigmaroles of decision. She has to assess all the negatives before she gets near to a positive. Basically, she's just afraid of anything new. She hasn't been to Turkey before. So she's scared she'll make a fool of herself in unfamiliar surroundings.'

'I think you're right. How's the Sauvignon?'

'Delicious.'

'I thought you'd agree. They do some very clever things with their wines in New Zealand. Anyway, how come you've got this holiday coming up?'

'A friend's offered me the use of his villa in a village called Kayaköy.'

'Useful friend to have. Or was this for "services rendered"?' Ted suggested roguishly.

'I beg your pardon?'

'Another of all these ex-lovers that Carole goes on about?'

'No,' Jude lied. 'He's a guy called Barney Willingdon.'

'Oh.' Clearly, the name meant something to Ted.

'Property developer,' said Jude.

'Yes, I know.'

'You've met him?'

'No, I haven't, actually, but I've heard a lot about him.'

'How come?'

'One of the advantages, Jude – or disadvantages, according to your personality – of being a pub landlord is that a lot of people talk to you.'

'And in your case is it an advantage or disadvantage?'

'Depends who's doing the talking. You do get some interesting people passing through. You also get your regulars who bore you to death with the same moans every night. Hazard of a publican's life. I've got a mate who runs a pub in London. He has his end of the bar where he always stands when he's not serving, and over it he's got this big sign saying "NO SYMPATHY CORNER".'

'Ooh, I love that. Maybe you should do the same, Ted?'

'Don't think I haven't thought of it.'

'Anyway, what's this got to do with Barney Willingdon?'

'Ah, well now, you see, his name is heard quite often round here.'

'Oh?'

'There's a guy who used to work with him who's one of my regulars.'

'One of the interesting ones or the moaners?'

'Can't you tell from my tone of voice?'

'Yes, I certainly can.'

'Name of Fergus McNally.' Ted Crisp looked at his watch. 'He'll be in here soon. On the dot of six every night. You'd recognize him. But you're not often in here at six. Nobody is, so I'm the one who gets buttonholed. Talk about a captive audience. It's like I'm nailed to the bloody bar with Fergus till I get a few more customers in.'

'So you never escape?'

'Only if I can fob him off on some other poor bugger and let him bore them to death instead.'

'Ted, this may sound a strange request, but could I volunteer to be "some other poor bugger"?'

FOUR

Fergus McNally contrived to look like a rougher version of Barney Willingdon. Both were in their fifties, large and bearded, but whereas the owner of Chantry House glowed with success, around Fergus McNally hung the sour aroma of disappointment. Even if Ted Crisp had not prepared her, and before the new arrival had even opened his mouth, Jude would have identified him as a moaner.

He ordered 'the usual', and Ted pulled him a pint of Sussex Gold. Fergus's accent was also Sussex, quite similar to Barney's. Maybe they were both local boys.

Then, still with a residue of bewilderment at Jude's request, Ted Crisp introduced them.

'Do you live in Fethering too, Fergus?' asked Jude.

'Oh yes. One of my rules of life has always been: live near enough to a pub so that you can walk home, whatever state you're in.' For no very good reason he let out a hearty chuckle. 'You imply you do as well.'

'Yes. Down the High Street.'

'Oh, I probably know the house . . .?' suggested Fergus.

But Jude didn't pick up the cue to volunteer any further information. She'd already identified Fergus McNally as the kind of man it might be difficult to shake off. Ted Crisp, glad to be off the hook, sidled down to the other end of the bar where he picked up a cloth and started assiduously drying dry glasses.

Fergus had perched on a bar stool, so Jude also drew one up and sat beside him.

'Ted said your name's Jude. Jude what?'

'People just call me Jude.'

'Well, everyone calls me Fergus. Fortunately, nobody's ever tried to shorten it. I don't fancy going through life called "Gus".'

'Or "Fer".'

'Nobody'd ever call anyone "Fer",' he said, slightly puzzled. Jude got the impression that a sense of humour was not one of his major qualities. 'Well, this is a nice surprise,' he went on.

'What is?'

'Meeting you. Normally, when I come in of an evening I have to put up with Ted's moaning. God, he does go on about stuff. It's not often that I'm introduced to a dishy woman.'

There was something stiff and clumsy about the way he made the compliment. Whether or not he realized it, Fergus McNally was not a natural ladies' man.

'Do you work round here too?' he went on.

'I work from home. I'm a healer.'

He looked duly surprised. 'Right. So if I'm suffering from some ghastly illness, I come to you and you lay your hands on me, do you? Sounds rather good.'

Jude didn't like the way he said 'lay your hands', so she moved the conversation on. 'What do you do, Fergus?'

'Very little, I'm afraid, at the moment,' he replied, moving into self-pitying mode. 'I used to be in property.'

'What aspect of property?'

'Development. Had my own company. But then the recession came, and . . .' He shrugged and downed the remains of his pint. It hadn't lasted very long. He gestured to Jude's glass. 'You ready for another?'

'Just a small one to top it up.'

'What is it?'

Jude had to stop the instinctive reply of 'Chilean Chardonnay' and said, 'A New Zealand Sauvignon Blanc.'

Fergus summoned Ted from his redundant glass polishing and gave the order. While he served the drinks the landlord flashed a covert, *'What did I tell you?'* look to Jude. Then he escaped back to the other end of the bar.

They moved to a small alcove to sit, and Jude picked up the conversation where they'd left off. 'Yes, the recession was tough on lots of small businesses, wasn't it?'

But that offended Fergus. 'Mine wasn't a small business. It was international. I'd got developments all over. And would have had a lot more if it hadn't all gone belly up.'

'What was the problem? Banks refusing to give you credit?'

'Well, it came to that in the end, of course. But it wasn't what started the rot.'

Jude was silent, confident that she was going to get Fergus McNally's long sad saga whether she wanted it or not.

'No, basically I was shafted,' he went on. 'Should have stayed on my own.'

'You went into partnership with someone else?' asked Jude, rather suspecting she knew in which direction the conversation was moving.

'Yes, and he turned out to be a complete bastard.'

'Ah.'

'Screwed me totally. Ruined my life. At the end of it I was bankrupt and my marriage had broken up. Had to sell the big house and all our personal property abroad. That's why I've ended up in a tatty rented flat in Fethering of all godforsaken places.'

There was an inevitability about what was about to be said, so Jude asked the question sooner rather than later. 'What was your partner's name?'

And sure enough the reply came: 'Barney Willingdon.'

'Ah.'

'You sound as if you know him.'

'We have met, yes,' replied Jude, offering no further elaboration.

'Well, when you next see him, you can tell him from me that he's a total bastard and I'll get my own back on him one day!'

'I'm unlikely to see him again,' Jude lied. 'What actually happened?'

'Barney and I had known each other from kids – even went to the same bloody primary school in Worthing. Separate ways after that, but we both ended up in the property business. Both started out locally, Barney buying up big houses and turning them into retirement homes, while I was developing student accommodation in Brighton. We'd bump into each other occasionally, all perfectly pleasant. We were kind of rivals but not really, because we were in such different areas of the business. Just a bit of one-upmanship about which one of us was making more dosh. And we were both doing all right back then. Late eighties, early nineties it was hard to go wrong in property. And then Barney and I both got involved abroad. I was building holiday villas in Spain, he was more Eastern Mediterranean.'

'Turkey?'

'Yes. He started there, building in the Fethiye area. He flew me out a few times to see if I wanted to invest. Sadly, at that point I didn't have any spare cash. Otherwise I would have done quite well out of it. But Barney's kind of restless when it comes to his business, he always wants to be moving on, always thinks there's a bigger pay day just around the corner. So he started to get involved in Northern Cyprus. He said it was a free-for-all out there, everyone coining it. And then one day Barney asked me out for lunch and put a proposition to me.'

There was a silence. Jude waited.

'It was on a completely different scale from individual villas on the Turkish mainland. Barney had this really big scheme in mind, whole valley full of holiday apartments to the east of Kyrenia. He'd got local Turkish partners – you can't do business out there without that – but he needed more investment. And at that lunch I tell him my business has really taken off and this time, yes, I might have some cash to invest.

'Next thing I know I'm being flown out to Northern Cyprus, put up in one of his luxury villas. I'm meeting Barney's local partners, I'm shown the apartment builds they've already done, I'm looking at the site where the new development's going to be. I'm meeting British expats who're telling me what a fabulous lifestyle they have out there. And it is a great place, proper Mediterranean holiday island. Lovely beaches, restaurants, diving, other sea sports – great. And enough archaeological sites for people who like that kind of thing. These bloody great Crusaders' castles. It's a fabulous place, and property's a lot cheaper there than it is in other parts of the Med.

'Well, it all looks bloody rosy, I can tell you, and pretty soon I announce to Barney that I'm in. I accept his deal, it all goes to the lawyers, everything sorted out, we're partners.'

'What, the two companies merge?'

'No, it wasn't like that, but it was a closer arrangement than me just investing in his mainland villas. We're partners on the one project, the Northern Cyprus development, that's it. And at first everything goes fine. Building work starts – and with it a blooming great marketing campaign, selling the apartments to the Brits.'

'Always the Brits. No Turkish?'

'No, Turks don't want to live in places like that. This was strictly holiday accommodation, and if you can fill it you're on to a real money-spinner. Anyway, these apartments are being snapped up off-plan like there's no tomorrow. Future's looking even rosier for Barney and me.'

Gloom encroached further on to his face. Jude noticed that his glass was empty. 'Get you another?'

Fergus McNally consented, too preoccupied to realize it wasn't strictly speaking her turn. At the bar, as he filled clean glasses for them, Ted Crisp murmured to Jude, 'Got on to the subject of his business partner yet?'

'Oh yes.'

'Then you could be there a while. I've got a camp bed out the back if you find you need it.'

She returned to the alcove, handed over Fergus's pint and encouraged him to continue.

He was more than happy to pick up the cue. 'Well, what we get next is political problems. I mean, I don't know if you understand the status of Northern Cyprus, as it were, internationally?'

'Remind me.'

'The place is not quite a rogue state, but it's as near as dammit. It's only recognized by Turkey. Lot of Turkish soldiers stationed there. This all happened after an invasion by the Turks – 1974 I think it was. Before then there'd been a mix of Greek Cypriots and Turkish Cypriots in the area. After the invasion, most of the Greeks went south to the bit that's part of Greece and a lot of Turkish Cypriots came up north. So there's now two states with a border between them – well, actually there's a United Nations buffer zone that goes right through the middle of Nicosia.

'I don't want to bore you with politics, Jude, but there've

been lots of initiatives to get Cyprus reunified. And they've got stronger as Turkey's become keen to join the European Union. The existence of this unrecognized state of Northern Cyprus has been a bit of a stumbling block there.

'Needless to say, the uncertainty over the place's future has an effect on everything, particularly the property business. There are disputes over ownership of a lot of land there. The Greek Cypriots were turfed out, see, but if there is reunification there's a strong possibility they might come back and claim their old property. And when we talk about property we're talking about the land, regardless of what's been subsequently built on it. Foreign buyers could find themselves owning a property but not owning the land on which it's built. So, you see, there's a lot of confusion over who owns what – or who will own what in the future.'

'So is the land where you and Barney were building your apartments disputed territory?'

'Potentially, yes. Not, of course, that he told me that when he's all chummy trying to get me involved.'

'And is that why the whole thing went belly up?'

'One of the reasons. First, there's something in the news about an English couple who've bought on Greek-owned land and face the prospect of having their property demolished, and that's the kind of rumour which doesn't do a lot for public confidence. It's not exactly an incentive for people to buy in Northern Cyprus, is it? And then, of course, you get the financial crisis and the banks stop lending and nobody's got any money and . . .'

'But surely,' said Jude, 'Barney Willingdon would be suffering from all that just as much as you did?'

'You'd think so, wouldn't you? But oh no. He's a shifty bastard, and his lawyers are even shiftier. And there was something dodgy going on with his Northern Cypriot partners too. Result of it all is that Barney gets out of all responsibility for the development of the apartments, and I'm landed with the full costs for everything.'

'But that must've been illegal, mustn't it?'

'Not as it turned out, no. Like I say, he's got very shifty lawyers. And mine, I regret to say, were way too honest. And slow. And, now I come to think of it, bloody stupid. Couple of clauses they didn't pick up on, and there am I, shafted – but totally legally. I have no redress through the courts. I just have to face the music on my own. Which led to me being made bankrupt, losing my house and—'

'Yes, you told me everything that happened.' Jude's sympathy for Fergus McNally was not total. She got the impression that, given the opportunity – and brighter lawyers – he'd have been quite capable of pulling the same kind of deception on Barney. But nonetheless she did say, 'I'm sorry.'

'So am I – bloody sorry! And in time Barney Willingdon's going to be bloody sorry too!'

'But you say he didn't do anything illegal?'

'No, no, he's far too clever for that. Like I said, I can't get at him through the courts. But that doesn't mean I won't be revenged on him somehow.' Fergus took a long swallow of beer and then said, with almost frightening intensity, 'I'll get the bastard.'

'Are you talking physical violence?' asked Jude.

'No. I hope I won't be reduced that that. Not that I wouldn't take great pleasure in bashing the bastard's face in. But I'd rather get him to experience the kind of public humiliation I've had to go through.'

'You don't have the means of bankrupting him, do you?'

'No. I've been doing some research into his background, though. The Northern Cyprus apartments aren't the first dodgy deal he's been associated with.'

'But he'd probably have covered his tracks legally in other cases as well.'

'Yes, but there are a few other people he shafted before me. Both in this country and in Turkey. I've been making contact with them, and they're all more than happy to dish the dirt on Barney Willingdon.'

'Presumably, they can't get him on a legal charge any more than you can?'

'Maybe not. But there's one guy in particular called Kemal . . .'

'Turkish?'

'Yes. One of the former partners out there. He's got some very interesting personal stuff on Barney.'

'Oh? How do you mean – personal?'

'Have you met his wife?'

'Henry? Yes.'

'Well, she is the number two model.'

'I got that impression.'

'And what happened to number one model, Zoë, was very interesting.'

'Oh?'

'She died in an accident . . .'

'Right.'

'Or rather she died in something that appeared to be an accident.'

'Meaning?'

'Meaning that this guy I met, Kemal, is pretty convinced that Barney engineered that accident. That he actually murdered his first wife.'

FIVE

Jude was troubled by her encounter with Fergus McNally, who incidentally wouldn't elaborate further on his reasons for suspecting his former partner of being a murderer. Either Kemal hadn't told him the circumstances of the first wife's death or Fergus was keeping the details to himself. She knew she'd been listening to the ramblings of a disappointed man with an axe to grind, but some of the things he'd said about Barney had struck chords with her. Back at the time when they had had their affair (the one that Carole must never find out about), she'd recognized Barney as a chancer – and that had, indeed, been part of his appeal. And it had also been part of the reason why she'd chosen to end the relationship. Though she'd found him charming and sexy – and enjoyed his spontaneous craziness – at a very basic level there was something she didn't trust about him. She also knew that his business ethics had been at least as dodgy as the ones he followed in his personal life.

And, though the affair had been a long time ago, before either of them was married for the first time, Jude still didn't have total trust in Barney Willingdon. Now surrounded by the trappings of success with his beautiful Mark Two wife, he remained a chancer. Close to the wind was his natural habitat.

Jude also wondered whether the stress-related back pain for which she had treated Henry Willingdon reflected the strain of sharing her husband's life of perpetual risk-taking. The perfection of Chantry House might present the ultimate image of security, but Jude knew that no one living with Barney Willingdon would ever feel completely safe. Henry might appear to have him under her thumb, but he was elusive, a hard man to pin down.

Whether Barney Willingdon was capable of having murdered his first wife was, however, another matter altogether. There, Jude thought, Fergus McNally's animus against his former partner had just got out of control.

The suggestion was an intriguing one, though. Jude wouldn't mind finding out more about the circumstances of the first Mrs Willingdon's death.

But any investigation she did conduct was another thing that must be kept a secret from Carole. Her neighbour was already sufficiently ambivalent about the holiday in Turkey. If there was any suggestion that they were there enjoying the hospitality of a murderer, Jude could all too readily predict Carole's reaction.

Though, actually, she thought she already knew Carole's decision about the whole holiday idea. Turkey was just too far out of her neighbour's comfort zone for her to think seriously of going there. Jude went to bed that night, expecting the next day to bring a resounding no from Carole.

It was the telephone that woke her. 'Hello,' she said, a little blearily.

'Just to say I've confirmed them.' Carole's voice was strong, almost bouncy.

'Confirmed what?'

'Well, the flights to Dalaman, obviously.'

'Oh. Really? Well. Good.' Jude tried to assemble the diffuse parts of her brain. 'Is this for a week or a fortnight?'

'A fortnight. The trouble with just a week is that you don't relax properly. By the time you've untwitched you're starting to worry about the return journey.' Carole apparently didn't find anything odd about repeating Jude's words back to her almost verbatim as she went on cheerily, 'We'll have to make quite an early start on the Monday, but if we catch the five fifty train from Fethering, we'll be at Gatwick in time.'

'Or we could just get a cab,' Jude suggested.

'No, we don't want any unnecessary expenditure,' said Carole quite sharply. Her words reminded Jude that the two of them had rather different attitudes to money. These had really been of little significance when the issue had only been who bought the drinks in the Crown and Anchor, but might feature more forcibly when the two of them were spending a whole fortnight together.

'Anyway, I must get on,' continued Carole. 'Quite a lot to sort out if we're off a week today.'

'Oh, there's not that much to do,' said Jude, whose holiday preparations would only involve chucking a few garments into a suitcase and ensuring that she had an adequate supply of trashy poolside books.

'Well, I've got a lot to do,' said Carole primly. 'Not least finding a suitable kennels for Gulliver.'

'Isn't there one you've used before?'

'No. If I go to Stephen and Gaby's I take him with me. Since I've been in Fethering I haven't been away and had to leave him.'

This brought home to Jude what a big deal going away was for Carole. And made her feel a little more forgiving of her neighbour's vacillation. 'So what suddenly made you decide?' she asked.

'Decide what?'

'Decide that you would go to Turkey with me?'

'Oh,' said Carole airily, 'I'd decided that as soon as the idea was mentioned.'

Something snapped in Jude. Uncharacteristically splenetic, she demanded, 'Then why the hell didn't you tell *me*?'

*   *   *

The two women's preparations during the next week were very different. Jude, who didn't really need any holiday planning, was kept busy with work. Because of going away at short notice there were appointments for her healing services that had to be postponed or, in more cases, fitted in before she left. She was a soft touch with her regular clients and soon found that she was booked up right through to the end of the Sunday. She would certainly need the break by the time they left for Dalaman on the Monday morning.

Carole's approach was, of course, different and involved a lot of time researching on her laptop. (Having for a long time resisted the allure of computers, she now spent hours a day googling. Never for trivial things though. Carole Seddon didn't believe in time-wasting.)

Her first task was, as she'd said, to find suitable accommodation for Gulliver. Though she wasn't one to be soppy about animals, she felt a strong sense of duty towards her Labrador and wanted to ensure that he was put up in a reputable establishment. So she assiduously googled 'Dog Boarding Kennels', eliminating some on grounds of distance and others on details that she didn't like on their websites, until she came up with a shortlist of four. These she contacted, but rather than making the choice and immediately booking online, being Carole Seddon, she arranged to visit all four – with Gulliver – before reaching her decision.

If she'd hoped the dog might express some preference, she was disappointed. But he clearly knew something upsetting was about to happen, and at each of the four kennels he fixed her with the same expression of betrayed reproach.

When they returned to High Tor, after trying to assuage her guilt by giving Gulliver a dog biscuit, Carole went straight up to the spare bedroom where her computer lived. (Though she was aware that one of the advantages of a laptop was its mobility, guided by some Calvinist proscription of mixing business with pleasure, she never worked on it anywhere else in the house.) Online, she made the booking at the kennels she had selected (with no help from Gulliver). Having never before made a comparable transaction, she was a little shocked by how much it cost. Though they were getting the use of

Morning Glory for nothing, Carole still felt a little guilt at
how much the additional costs of the holiday might be. Paying
for the flights on her credit card had taken a substantial sum,
and Jude hadn't yet given her the promised cheque for her
share. She had a Carole Seddon moment (and she would have
more before their departure) of wondering whether the trip to
Turkey was such a good idea after all.

Then there was the matter of clothes. Carole didn't enjoy
any kind of clothes shopping, though in recent years, since
Lily had been born, she had derived a lot of pleasure from
buying garments for her granddaughter. But as a general rule,
Carole reckoned buying clothes for herself was self-indulgent.
It was not an experience she enjoyed, and her aim in what
she wore was to be as anonymous as possible. She favoured
light browns and white and navy (she remembered her mother
saying, 'You'll never go wrong with white and navy.'). During
her working life at the Home Office she had worn a lot of
black, but since then black had got dangerously trendy and
made too much of a statement for Carole Seddon. So she
didn't wear it any more.

But one thing that she knew from her online reading was that
Turkey could be very hot, possibly too hot for Carole's existing
summer wardrobe. She might have to purchase some cotton
tops (definitely not T-shirts) and trousers (definitely not jeans).

And then there was the terrifying matter of a bathing
costume. Though she had lived a good few years in Fethering
and walked daily on the beach with Gulliver, Carole had never
actually been in the sea there, not even to paddle. But she did
nonetheless have a bathing costume. It had been bought one
summer when she had rented a beach hut at the nearby village
of Smalting. The aim of the exercise had been to have somewhere in which to entertain her granddaughter Lily and, after
the distractions of a murder investigation, the two of them had
had a very successful week together.

But the costume she had bought then had been a one-piece
in, to Carole's mind, a rather daring red, and from some of
the things she had read online she wondered whether it was
suitable apparel for a Muslim country. Maybe something less
flamboyant would be more appropriate.

Having reached this conclusion, Carole Seddon set off in her Renault, without enthusiasm, for the Marks & Spencer's in Chichester.

The navy-blue swimming costume she bought was of the kind that a nun would not have felt out of place on a beach in. She also, rather daringly, purchased a pair of beige cotton shorts, though she thought it extremely unlikely she would wear them. It was many years since Carole Seddon's legs had last been seen in public.

Because she would be in Chichester, Carole had also taken a carefully prepared list for a major shopping raid on Boots. Although she had no intention of baring much flesh in Kayaköy, she purchased suntan lotions of various strengths from Factor Fifty downwards. Also after-sun and cold cream. Plasters in various sizes, cotton wool, insect repellent, Anthisan, Savlon, Nurofen and paracetamol (just to be sure). And, of course, Imodium. (One of the online sites said there were a lot of kebabs likely to be served up in Turkey, and Carole Seddon had a deep mistrust of kebabs.)

Boots was followed by an electrical gadgetry shop, where she bought adaptor plugs that would fit Turkish sockets. Once in there, a pure victim of marketing, she also bought a 'universal all-in-one mobile phone charger' – though her firm intention was, despite taking her phone with her, not to use it except in the direst emergencies. She'd heard terrible stories about the draconian 'roaming charges' that could be incurred by incautious mobile phone users abroad.

As well, although she had already done a lot of research online, she went to Waterstones and bought the *Rough Guide to Turkey* along with a large map of the Turkish coast. And then she devoted all her spare time to finding out more about the country.

She concentrated first on Turkey's history and, being Carole Seddon, approached it like someone mugging up their Specialist Subject for an appearance on *Mastermind*. By the time she and Jude left for Dalaman, Carole could have answered questions on the Hittites and the First Anatolian empire, the funerary monuments of the Lycians, the Battle of

Kadesh, Cyrus the Great, Roman domination, the Macedonian Dynasty, the Janissaries, Süleyman the Magnificent and the modernizing achievements of Kemal Atatürk.

Carole Seddon had always had qualities of a completist.

On Friday evening the phone rang in Woodside Cottage. Jude was exhausted after a day of back-to-back healing sessions. The effort of concentration always left her drained.

'Hello?'

'Oh, it's Barney.'

Jude wondered why he was ringing. They'd had a fairly exhaustive conversation earlier in the week about the practical details of the forthcoming fortnight at Morning Glory – keys, the electrical system, numbers for the pool man and the plumber, advice on the best supermarket in Kayaköy. Still, maybe there was some minor item he had forgotten to mention.

So, indeed, it proved. Barney told her that his ex-holiday-rep friend Nita Davies was going to meet them at the airport. He wanted to check the time their flight got in.

'That's very kind of her. Are you sure she won't mind?'

'Don't worry about Nita,' said Barney airily. 'She owes me a few favours. She's happy to do it. Besides, while she's driving you from Dalaman to Morning Glory she can fill you in a bit about the local area.'

'That'd be great,' said Jude. 'Thank you very much for fixing it.'

'No problem. Like I say, I can fix anything out there,' said Barney. 'Anything you need, just give me a call on the mobile.'

'Thanks very much.' And Jude gave him the details of their flight to Dalaman.

But then it became clear that obtaining practical information was not the only reason for Barney's call. He sounded as bouncy as ever, but there was something almost surreptitious about his ebullience. 'Jude, I just wanted to say that I will be out in Turkey during the time you're there.'

'Oh? Yes, you said you might be. Are you telling me that you're going to need Morning Glory after all?'

'Heavens, no. I've got plenty of other places to stay out there.'

'Good. Well, Carole and I will look forward to seeing you.'

'I will very much look forward to seeing *you*.' The way he said it sounded warning bells.

'Oh?'

'Listen, Jude . . .' His voice became deeper, more intimate. 'It's been really great seeing you again.'

'It's been nice to see you,' she said cautiously.

'When you came to the house last week with your friend, I was just blown away.'

'By Carole? She'll be very flattered,' said Jude, hoping to joke her way out of what was about to come.

'No, of course not by Carole. By you, Jude. It just all came back to me, how much we meant to each other all that time ago. Don't you feel the same?'

'My recollection,' she replied carefully, 'is that yes, we had a very good couple of months, which I look back on with pleasure. But it was a long time ago, and a lot has happened since. We've both been married twice, for one thing. You still are married.'

'Yes, but things haven't been working out with Henry recently.'

'I don't want to hear anything about that, Barney. Presumably Henry's not going out to Turkey with you?'

'No. Which is all the more reason why you and I—'

'Look, Barney, if you're going to come on to me while we're out in Turkey, then we may as well pull the plug on the whole idea of going there – right now.'

'Jude, I wouldn't put you under any pressure to do anything you didn't want to do.'

'Good. I'm very glad to hear it.'

'It's just the thought of us both being out there at the same time and . . . well, it would be good to get together.'

'I'm sure we will. Meet for a meal or something. But you seem to be forgetting, amongst other things, that I'll have Carole with me.'

'I'm sure you'd be able to get away from her for the odd hour.'

'You don't know Carole. She hangs on like a Rottweiler,' said Jude, again trying to neutralize Barney's advances with flippancy.

'Jude, look, we're both grown-ups. And I've got to an age when, if I feel an attraction for someone, I—'

'Stop it, Barney. May I make it entirely clear to you that nothing is going to happen between us in Turkey?'

'You say that now, but it's a very romantic place. When we get out there . . .'

'When we get out there nothing will have changed. And, Barney, will you please promise me that you will not come on to me at any point while we're in Kayaköy?'

'Very well,' he said grudgingly. But in his voice there was another tone Jude recognized of old. Barney Willingdon was one of the most cocksure men she had ever met. It never occurred to him that any woman he fancied might not recip-rocate his feelings. And, to her considerable annoyance, she found that she did still feel a small tug of attraction towards him.

His phone call unsettled her. The trip to Turkey and Barney's generous offer of the use of Morning Glory had all seemed so straightforward. But now it had become potentially compli-cated. It's true, Jude thought ruefully, there is no such thing as a free lunch.

She was also annoyed with herself for not posing some questions to Barney about something else while she'd had the opportunity. She'd liked to have asked him what happened to his first wife, Zoë . . .

SIX

Carole Seddon spent the Sunday before they left ticking things off the many lists she had made. Her tasks included taking Gulliver to the kennels she had chosen for him. The look of reproach he cast upon her as they parted made her feel as if she had been solely responsible for the Massacre of the Innocents.

Back at High Tor, Carole faced the decision of whether or not to take her laptop with her to Turkey. It was heavy, it was a potential target for thieves and it never under normal circumstances strayed from the spare room. But then again she was sometimes shocked by how much she relied on the machine. So many things were so easily googleable. And she wouldn't like to be out of email contact with Stephen, Gaby and Lily. She decided she would take it. Besides, Barney had said that Morning Glory had broadband connectivity. The laptop would go in her hand baggage. So another item was ticked off a list.

And in between her packing and panicking, Carole brushed up on the handy phrases in Turkish which she had found online. She didn't bother with how the words were written, concentrating instead on the phonetic pronunciations that were listed. Carole cracked 'yes' and 'no' first. They were respectively 'ev-et' and 'hi-ear'. She felt fairly confident of greeting people with 'mare-ha-ba' which meant 'hello', but found that saying goodbye was more complicated. It depended on whether you were the person leaving or the person being left. The former said 'hosh-ch-kal', while the latter had to say 'guu-leh guu-leh'. 'Please' was 'lut-fen', and 'thank you' 'te-sh-qu-err ed-err-im'. More useful, Carole reckoned, would be 'I don't speak Turkish' ('turk-jeh bill-mi-yor-um'), 'Do you speak English?' ('inn-gliz-je con-nush-or mus-un-us') and, most useful of all, 'I don't understand' ('si-zi ann-la-ma-yor-um').

But, search as she might, she couldn't find the Turkish for the vital question, 'Do you sell Imodium?'

Carole's bags had been packed and repacked many hours before Jude started to think what she was going to take to Morning Glory. For her, the Sunday was a day of back-to-back healing sessions, which left her completely wiped out. When she said goodbye to her last client it was seven thirty in the evening. Before pouring herself a large drink and getting something to eat (she hadn't had time for lunch), she checked for messages on her mobile phone. There was one, from Henry Willingdon, asking her to ring back.

Some final housekeeping detail about the villa, Jude supposed. She was wrong.

As soon as she got through, Henry said very directly, 'I just wanted to warn you. Don't get involved with Barney.'

'Don't worry. I'm not going to. Getting involved with Barney is the last thing on my mind.'

'He flew out to Turkey this morning. He's going there because of you.' There was a lot of tension behind the upper-class vowels.

'He's not going there because of me. I assume he's got business out there.'

'That's just a smokescreen. It's you he wants to see.'

'I'm sure that's not the case,' said Jude, feeling rather wretched.

'It is. I know Barney. I saw the way he looked at you when you came to the house. He thinks picking up with a girlfriend from long ago will make him feel young again.'

'I would have thought it would have the reverse effect, make him even more aware of the passage of the years, seeing how much we've both changed.'

'So you're *admitting* the two of you might pick up again?'

'No, I'm not,' said Jude wearily, wishing she hadn't got into the position of owing any kind of favour to Barney Willingdon.

'If anything does happen while you're out in Kayaköy, I'll hear about it! I have contacts out there.'

'Henry, your contacts can watch me twenty-four/seven. They will not see anything inappropriate happening between me and Barney.'

'I know that he phoned you on Friday.'

'I'm not about to deny it.'

'And he wasn't just phoning you about practical details for your stay at Morning Glory.'

'I don't deny that either.'

'He said that he wanted to pick up your relationship, didn't he?'

'Yes, he did. And I told him there was no chance of that happening.'

'Hm. Barney can be very persistent.'

'I know he can. But over the years I've got quite good at dealing with persistent men. I'm strong enough and grown-up enough to resist any advances Barney might make to me,' said Jude, hoping her words were true.

'Just be careful,' said Henry. 'He likes getting his own way.'

'Yes, I remember that.'

'And he's also very good at getting his own way.'

'Not with me he won't be.'

'And when Barney doesn't get his own way, he can turn very nasty indeed.'

'I remember that too. It was one of the many reasons why I had to break off our relationship.'

'Don't forget what happened to Zoë.'

'His first wife?'

'Yes. That was in Turkey. So, Jude, you just be very careful.'

'What actually did happen to Zoë?' Jude asked.

But Henry Willingdon had rung off.

SEVEN

Needless to say, Carole won about their transport to Gatwick. Jude would much rather have shared a cab. Then she could feel like she was on holiday from the moment she left Woodside Cottage. Whereas going by rail involved getting up earlier, dragging their bags to the station, waiting about for the train to arrive (Carole had, needless to say, ensured that they arrived far too early), then dragging the bags again from the train to the terminal – and reversing the process when they returned home.

But Carole had said they would catch the 5.50 from Fethering station and so it was the 5.50 from Fethering station that they caught. Carole had two suitcases and a shoulder bag; Jude had a holdall and a small knapsack. Jude was dressed in a bright skirt and a T-shirt. She felt a bit cold, but didn't want to be weighed down with a bulky cardigan which she knew she'd never wear once when they were out in Turkey.

Carole was dressed in navy trousers and a grey jacket over a white shirt. On top of this she wore her Burberry raincoat.

Jude knew that that too would not be worn once during their holiday, but she made no comment. She thought there might be other things over which they disagreed in the next two weeks, but she didn't want to start the fortnight with an argument.

Jude had got a suitably trashy novel in her knapsack, but she felt too dozy and exhausted to start reading it on the train. Time enough for lots of reading by the infinity pool at Morning Glory.

Carole had, of course, stopped the delivery of her papers. 'Did you do that, Jude?'

'No.'

'Oh dear. Think of the waste.'

'I didn't do it, Carole, because, as you might have noticed by now, I don't have papers delivered. When I want to read a newspaper, I go out and buy one.'

'Oh.'

They'd left too early for Carole to get a *Times* from the newsagent, but she had a book of *Times* crosswords in her shoulder bag, and during the journey to Gatwick she focused intently on one of those.

Theirs was a charter flight and, in the way of charter flights, once they had arrived at the airport and checked in their bags they found it was delayed by two hours.

'Oh dear,' said Carole, on the verge of panic mode. 'That'll spoil all our plans, won't it?'

'No, it just means we'll get there two hours later than we thought we would. That is, assuming there isn't a further delay.'

'Is that likely?' asked Carole anxiously.

'You never know with charter flights. Quite possible. But we may get lucky and it'll only be two hours.'

'I don't know how you can describe a two-hour flight delay as "getting lucky".'

'Well, it's just one of those things,' said Jude. 'Nothing we can do about it.'

'But don't you feel infuriated by the fact that we can't do anything about it?' Throughout her life Carole had always hated not feeling in control.

'No, of course not,' said Jude with complete honesty. 'Some things just happen.'

'Oh, and I suppose you just disappear into some transcendental Zen state and nothing gets to you?'

Jude grinned. 'No, I just accept that sometimes things go wrong.'

'Huh,' said Carole Seddon, as only she could say the word.

'Oh, come on, let's go and get some breakfast,' said Jude.

'We get a meal on the flight,' said Carole. 'We've paid for it.'

'Yes, but that doesn't change the fact that I feel very hungry *right now*.'

'Didn't you have anything to eat before you left?'

'God, no. At five in the morning my system is hardly functioning. Certainly not up to eating breakfast.'

'Oh.'

'You had something, I assume?'

'Just a bowl of muesli.'

'Come on, let's go and get something at Café Rouge.'

'I don't need to get something at Café Rouge.'

'Well, come and have a coffee and watch me while I have something at Café Rouge.'

Through Carole's head was proceeding a thought similar to the one Jude had had at the sight of the Burberry: there may be bigger issues ahead for us to disagree about, so don't let's have a disagreement yet. Carole did not wish to upset the apple cart at that point. Besides, she had been considerably cheered by the fact that she'd noticed an open W.H. Smith.

'Very well, Jude. I'll just go and get myself a *Times*, and I'll join you in there.'

'Fine.'

Though Café Rouge was allegedly of French inspiration, at the airport they were canny enough to offer a full English breakfast, and that was exactly what Jude felt like, so it was exactly what she ordered.

It had just been delivered when Carole returned, clutching her *Times*. 'Goodness, there was a big queue in Smith's.' She looked down at Jude's heaped plate. 'If you eat all that, you're never going to manage your meal on the plane.'

'You watch me,' said Jude. 'Anyway, I find while travelling you can eat a whole lot of different meals during the day without noticing.'

'Do you?'

'Yes. Something strange happens to one's metabolism. It's like drinking. You can pour the stuff down your throat on the plane and still feel perfectly sober when you pick up the hire car at the airport.'

'Can you?'

'Oh yes.'

'Then,' said Carole primly, 'I think it's a very good thing that we're getting a cab from Dalaman Airport.'

'Oh, but we're not.'

'What? But I've checked out where we get cabs from and the likely price.' Carole didn't like the prospect of her research being wasted. 'It's also very important that you agree a price with the taxi driver before you start the journey. According to the guidebook I read, some of the drivers are up to all kinds of scams.'

'We won't need a taxi. We're being met at the airport by Barney's holiday rep friend Nita Davies.'

'Oh? When did you hear that?'

'Friday, I think it was. Barney rang to tell me and, I'm sorry, I've just been so busy since then that I forgot to tell you.' Jude wondered whether that was strictly true, or was it just that she'd deliberately blanked the memory of that disquieting phone call from her mind?

'Well, that's very kind of her,' said Carole. But she wasn't sure about the news. While it appealed to the budgeting part of her mind because it would save the price of a cab from Dalaman Airport to Kayaköy, it also faced her with the prospect of meeting someone new. Carole Seddon always got worried about meeting new people, and she wished she'd had a bit more notice about meeting Nita in a few hours' time. What kind of English person, she wondered, chooses to spend her life in Turkey? And what kind of English person would get married to a Turk?

To the hovering waiter, Carole said she'd have a coffee. When offered the variety of coffees available, she said she'd just have an ordinary coffee.

'Regular filter?' asked the waiter.

'If that's what it's called, yes.'

'And nothing to eat?'

'No, thank you.' Though a croque-monsieur had just been delivered to an adjacent table, and it did look very tempting. But no, she'd had her five o'clock bowl of muesli. Ordering a second breakfast would be self-indulgent. It would, in fact, put her right on the edge of the slippery slope. And her path through life had seemed to have slippery slopes at every juncture. It wasn't easy being Carole Seddon.

When she'd mopped up the last bit of egg yolk with her last bit of toast, Jude called for the bill, which arrived almost instantaneously (the staff in the Gatwick Café Rouge were clearly used to people being suddenly summoned by flight boarding calls). As she drew out her credit card, Carole said, 'I should pay for my coffee.'

'I think I can afford to stand you a coffee.'

'Yes, but it's a matter of principle. If we're going to be spending the next fortnight together we must work out how we divide the bills.'

'I have thought about that,' said Jude. 'We should have a kitty.'

'A kitty?'

'Yes. I've even brought a special purse for the purpose.' Jude produced a purple leather one from her knapsack. 'We each put the same amount of money in here and use that to fund mutual purchases, like meals and food shopping.'

Carole was dubious. 'But what happens when that money runs out?'

'Then we put in more,' Jude explained, as if to a five-year-old. 'Again, we both put in exactly the same amount.'

Carole mentally – and sceptically – tested the proposal. And, to her surprise, couldn't find anything wrong with it. 'Well, that might work,' she conceded.

'It does work,' Jude asserted. 'It's what I've always done when I've gone on holiday with other friends.'

Carole didn't like having brought to her attention that she was just one in a sequence of friends with whom Jude had been on holiday, but she curbed her instinct to say anything. Nor did she argue further about paying for her regular filter coffee.

'Right.' As Jude gathered her belongings together, she looked at her watch. 'Let's just check there's no further delay to the flight.'

'Oh, do you think there might be?' asked Carole anxiously.

'We will only find out by looking at the departures board. And once we've done that, I'm going to hit the duty-free.'

'Why?' asked Carole.

'Because that is how one kills time at airports.'

'It's how they *want* you to kill time at airports,' said Carole sniffily. 'It's a blatant ploy to separate you from your money.'

'Well, with me it's a blatant ploy that usually works. I almost always end up buying something.'

'What?'

'I don't know until I see it, do I?'

'But is there anything you really *need*?' asked Carole.

A line from *King Lear* came unbidden into Jude's mind. '"Oh, reason not the need,"' she said. Carole's puzzled expression showed that the line hadn't come up in a *Times* crossword recently. 'Duty-free shopping,' Jude continued, 'is just an essential part of the airport experience.'

'Is it?' asked Carole. 'Well, I'll come round and look at things with you. But I'm not going to buy anything.'

'Fine. That is your prerogative.'

'Yes, it certainly is.'

'For me, it's part of going on holiday.'

'Is it?' repeated Carole, feeling once again dubious about the whole enterprise. Though she been Jude's neighbour for quite a long time, there were occasions when she felt she didn't really *know* her at all. And if their attitudes to the idea of duty-free shopping were so different, who could say what other points of variance might be discovered over the next two weeks?

There was no further delay to their flight registered on the departures board, so they 'hit the duty-free'. Jude picked up a perfume tester. Gucci Guilty.

'Is that what you usually buy?' asked Carole.

'No, I thought I'd try something different.'

'Oh,' said Carole, who had been using Elizabeth Arden Blue Grass for as long as anyone could remember.

Jude sniffed the spray on her wrist. 'Ooh, yes, I like that.'

'It's very expensive,' Carole observed, 'even with the duty off.'

'Yes, but I'm on holiday,' said Jude, once again prompting her neighbour to wonder how she ran her financial affairs.

Jude also bought a huge slab of fruit and nut chocolate and a bottle of Laphroaig malt whisky. 'For those balmy Turkish evenings.'

'Huh,' said Carole. And then, in spite of her earlier assertions, she also picked up something to buy. A small teddy bear sporting a pair of Union Jack shorts. Carole's attitude to buying things for her granddaughter Lily was completely different to how she considered buying things for herself.

The flight was uneventful, though a wait on the tarmac meant the plane actually left two hours and forty minutes after its scheduled departure. And Carole was extremely hungry by the time they were served their lunch. Which was minimal and not very nice.

While they were flying, Jude embarked on one of her trashy novels for a while, then after the meal she slept. Carole sat beside her, tense as a stick insect, and concentrated on that day's *Times* crossword. To her annoyance, there was one clue in the bottom-right corner that she couldn't for the life of her work out, and her irritation was increased by the knowledge that she probably wouldn't be able to get a paper the following day and check the solution.

Her mood was not improved by observing the other people on the flight. She saw tattoos and Union Jack T-shirts, which for Carole raised the spectre of the troubling word 'common'. Were the only people who went to Turkey lager-swilling yobs, she wondered.

And then she felt guilty for having bought Lily a teddy bear with Union Jack shorts. Was the national flag as 'common' on a teddy bear as it was on a T-shirt? This and other equally troubling questions circled round Carole Seddon's mind and, still unable to get the final clue, she tried to concentrate on the piece in *The Rough Guide to Turkey* about Lycian tombs. There were good examples of them at various sites, notably in the cliffs by the river at Dalyan, at Patara, Tlos, Fethiye and Pinara.

Carole wasn't particularly interested in archaeology, but she thought visiting tombs might be a good way of giving her some sense of purpose on the holiday.

When they stepped out of the plane at Dalaman Airport, the heat hit them almost like a physical blow. They followed the crocodile of other passengers to the air-conditioned oasis of the terminal building.

Once inside, everyone seemed to whip out their passports and rush towards a couple of what looked like ticket booths. 'What are they doing?' Carole asked Jude.

'Have to pay ten pounds for a visa to get into Turkey.'

'Really?' said Carole, who had not entered this sum into her detailed budgetary plans. 'That's daylight robbery.'

At the baggage reclaim it seemed, as it always does, that their bags were the last to emerge on to the carousel. Jude sat on the floor, serenely waiting, while Carole paced up and down, convinced that her luggage was on the way to Delhi.

There seemed to be no one in the customs control area as they walked through, and immediately they entered the airport foyer a voice said, 'Hi. You must be Carole and Jude.'

EIGHT

Nita was tall and blonde, dressed in a pale-blue sleeveless cotton top and white shin-length cotton trousers, with brown leather flip-flops. She looked very trim and tanned. Minimal make-up, just mascara and pale-pink lipstick. There was a thin gold chain around her neck and a chunky gold ring on her wedding finger.

Though she glowed with health, a slight crinkling around

her lips suggested that she was perhaps not as young as she appeared on first sight. But Nita looked supremely at ease in the alien environment into which Carole felt she had been thrust.

'How did you recognize us?' asked Jude.

Nita grinned. 'Barney gave me very full descriptions.'

Oh yes, thought Carole, I can imagine how he described me: thin, awkward, anxious-looking, unused to foreign travel. The Burberry over her arm seemed suddenly ridiculous, a blatant symbol of her insecurity and lack of *savoir faire*.

'And this is my friend Donna. Donna Lucas.' She indicated a shorter woman at her side. Dark-haired, well-rounded, the outline of a dark bikini top visible under her white polo shirt. 'Runs a restaurant in Hisarönü.'

'The Dirty Duck. Do come.' Donna's voice was pure, unreconstructed cockney. 'Full English Breakfast all day, Pub Favourites, Range of British Beers. And, what's more, special rates for friends of Nita's.' Whipping a couple of flyers out of her bag, she handed one to each of the new arrivals.

'Well, that sounds very nice,' said Carole politely, though what she'd read in her guidebook about Hisarönü didn't sound very nice at all.

'Ooh, sorry, must rush.' Donna Lucas was suddenly waving frantically. 'There's the person I'm picking up. Great to see you!' And with that she dashed off into the crowd.

'The car's parked just over there,' said Nita. 'Can I help you with one of those, Carole?'

'No, thank you, I'm fine,' came the instinctive response, though in fact pulling the two wheeled suitcases behind her while still keeping hold of her Burberry made her look rather clumsy. It also drew even more imagined attention to her from the oblivious Turks around the airport.

Again the move from air conditioning to direct sunlight was a shock as they walked towards the car park. Carole could feel herself beginning to sweat, though she knew it was from nerves rather than the heat. But it upset her. Sweating was something that Carole Seddon just didn't do.

Nita's car was a Hyundai Accent. Silver. In fact, looking round the car park, Carole observed that most of the cars were either silver or white. On the back window was the logo of a travel firm, so presumably it was the car that went with Nita's job. The boot was capacious enough for all their bags. Carole sat in the front, while Jude lolled dozily over the back seat. Now Jude felt she was genuinely on holiday and could begin to untwitch.

It would be a while, though, before Carole untwitched. Indeed, there was a question mark over whether Carole Seddon had ever in her life fully untwitched.

On the drive from Dalaman to Kayaköy, Nita demonstrated her background as a tour operator by keeping up a running commentary on sights they passed and the opportunities for tourism during their stay at Morning Glory. She did more of the second than the first because, although they went up and down some fairly impressive craggy mountains, the car stayed on the main D400 motorway and there weren't that many sights.

But there were unfamiliar images that made Carole feel she was definitely in a foreign country. They went past a few mosques, the domes and minarets of which reminded her of a copy of *The Arabian Nights* she'd had as a child. At the roadside there were stalls piled high with watermelons and oranges. Cafés offered a variety of goodies which, though written in the Roman alphabet, bore no relation to English words. Instinctively, because of her long acquaintance with the *Times* crossword, Carole found herself trying to make anagrams from them. One particular delicacy, *gözleme*, appeared with such frequency that she asked Nita what it meant.

'Pancakes. Kind of flatbread with fillings of meat, cheese or sometimes fruit or honey. Very good. Often in Turkish restaurants you see women in traditional dress squatting over big circular hotplates pouring out the batter and making endless *gözleme*. On menus with English translations you'll sometimes see them described as "village pancakes".'

'Oh, thank you.'

'You must try them.'

'Yes,' said Carole, not certain that she would. Did she really want to eat village pancakes? The whole concept of Turkish cuisine still rather worried Carole. In her mind she couldn't separate the word 'kebab' from the adjective 'dodgy'. And she felt glad she'd packed the Imodium.

Along the roadside they also passed a lot of posters attached to lamp posts or pasted to walls. Each featured large photographs of men with luxuriant moustaches.

'What are those about?' asked Carole.

'They're politicians. There's an election coming up.'

'Why have they all got moustaches?'

'I don't know,' said Nita, 'but it's very Turkish.'

'It looks as if it's more a competition between the moustaches than political parties.'

'You're not wrong. Turkish politics are extremely complicated. Probably easier just to vote for your favourite moustache.'

The car slowed down as they approached a row of toll booths. 'This is the tunnel,' Nita explained. 'You used to have to go right over the top of the mountain. This has cut a good half-hour out of the journey.'

But Nita didn't have to pay any money to have the barrier raised. The journey was clearly one she made so often that she had a season ticket.

Carole looked round into the back of the car. Jude was asleep. How could she be so relaxed in a country she didn't know, being driven by a person she didn't know? Carole felt a familiar pang of jealousy, knowing that she would never experience the insouciance that Jude so often exhibited.

Some way after the tunnel they turned off the D400, following the signs to Fethiye and Ölüdeniz. Nita drove with practised ease, knowing where she could speed up and when to slow down. In Fethiye, the road ran alongside the sea with rows of restaurants flanking it. There were a lot of yachts moored in a marina, their masts in serried ranks. 'Very popular with the sailing crowd, Fethiye,' said Nita. 'Are you into sailing, Carole?'

'No.' When she had been growing up, sailing, like skiing, was regarded by her parents as something rich people did.

'Or scuba diving? There's a lot of that out here.'

'No,' said Carole.

Traffic was heavy, and Carole's eyes were busy taking in the unfamiliar shop fronts, watching the people who wandered nonchalantly amidst the cars and vans. There were lots of scooters, driven by men without crash helmets and only flip-flops on their feet, who were buzzing around, threading their way through the bigger vehicles. The men wore jeans and T-shirts; the only ones in shorts were very obviously tourists. The women were also casually dressed; very few – and most of those were older – had their hair covered. Carole found herself wondering what it must feel like to be Muslim. Very odd to believe all that stuff. On the other hand, though she put 'C of E' on the diminishing number of forms that asked about her religion, Carole didn't believe in any of the Anglican stuff either. Very odd to have a faith was probably what she meant.

'There's a very good fish market here in Fethiye,' Nita went on. 'Circular place, surrounded by restaurants. You buy your fish in the central area, and then it's taken to one of the restaurants to be cooked. I recommend you do that for a lunch or dinner one day.'

'Thank you,' said Carole, though she didn't think she would. It sounded a rather complicated way of getting a meal, and it'd probably be very expensive too. Mind you, fresh fish might be safer than a kebab.

Up out of Fethiye, they took a narrow alley that looked hardly wide enough for a car. They turned right on to a wider road. Jolting on its uneven surface woke Jude up, just as Nita carefully steered round a large stone object in the middle of the road. It resembled a giant sentry box, maybe six feet square and fifteen feet high, with a roof shaped like a bishop's mitre.

'What the hell's that?' asked Jude blearily.

'It's a Lycian tomb.' Carole provided the answer before their guide had time to reply.

'Well done,' said Nita. 'You've certainly done your homework.'

'Actually, to be more accurate,' said Carole as they drove away from the memorial, 'it's a Lycian sarcophagus. The more traditional and distinctive Lycian tombs are carved out of rock

on cliff sides. There are examples all over the area, but perhaps
the best-known ones are to be found in Dalyan.'

'Right,' said Jude. Then, a little plaintively, 'Where have we
got to?'

'Just come through Fethiye,' said Nita. 'Another five miles
and we'll be in Kayaköy. And, incidentally—' she gestured
back towards the town – 'there's an example of a carved Lycian
tomb back there.'

The two visitors looked back and caught a glimpse of something rectangular carved out of a giant crag on the outskirts
of Fethiye. Then the car turned a corner and it was gone.

The road zigzagged up through a forest set on a steep hill. The
slickness with which Nita negotiated the many gear changes
again suggested this was a road she had travelled many times
before. Carole wasn't convinced that she would much enjoy
driving in Turkey if all the roads were like this one. And then,
of course, they drove on the right, which was an added compli-
cation. Maybe the car which Barney Willingdon had so carefully
insured for them would stay in the Morning Glory garage for
the entire next fortnight.

'How long have you known Barney, Nita?' asked Jude from
the back.

Carole would have felt embarrassed about asking such a
direct question to someone she'd only just met, but Nita didn't
seem to regard it as an intrusion. 'Oh, God knows. Must be
twenty years, I suppose. It was when I first came out here,
working for Thompson's. He wasn't building his luxury villas
then. Smaller developments, almost chalet style.'

'Have you ever actually worked for him?'

'No. I've always worked for one or other of the British
holiday companies, but inevitably we got to know most of the
developers. Back in those days there'd be lots of calls to Barney
about teething problems on the new builds. Showers not
working, toilets blocked. God, when I think of the number of
times I've been called to sort out a blocked toilet. Glamorous
job, this tour guide lark.'

'And you've been a tour guide all the time, have you?'
Carole dared to ask a question.

'Well, I have risen up the hierarchy a bit. More managerial

these days. And I'm working on more upmarket villas and
places. Though I still get to do my fair share of meeting
and greeting. And, if there's no one else round the office when
the call comes in, I still occasionally end up sorting out the
odd blocked toilet.'

'I gather,' Carole went on, emboldened, 'that Barney's going
to be coming out here soon . . .?'

'He's already here. Arrived yesterday.'

'But not with his wife this time,' Jude contributed.

'No.'

'Have you met Henry?'

'Of course I have.'

Carole and Jude both detected a slight caution in Nita's
voice.

'And did you meet his first wife,' Jude pressed on. 'Zoë?'

'Yes.'

'Do you know what actually happened to her?'

There was a silence. It could have occurred because Nita
was negotiating a particularly tight hairpin bend, or she could
have been deliberately avoiding a reply to Jude's question.
Either way, the moment for a reply had gone. They were going
steeply downhill now and, as they turned the corner, came out
of the trees' shade into full sunlight.

'There,' said Nita. 'Your first glimpse of Kayaköy.'

After the bustle of Fethiye, the sparsely wooded valley of
the village looked wonderfully flat and tranquil. Up against
the hills at the far end stood terraces of grey buildings, slightly
wobbly through the heat haze. 'Is that the ghost town?' asked
Jude.

'It certainly is.' The car turned another corner and the old
buildings disappeared from sight.

'And Morning Glory is actually in the village, is it?' asked
Carole. Though impressed by the quiet serenity of the scene
before them, she still worried about finding that their accommodation was surrounded by lager louts with tattoos and Union
Jack T-shirts.

'Oh yes. You'll see it in a minute. Fabulous views.'

'From here,' said Jude, 'the place doesn't look very
developed.'

'No. There are a lot of holiday villas and what-have-you, but they have been built quite sensitively. There are lots of restaurants too. The whole place is geared to the tourist trade, but wandering through the village you really wouldn't know it. You'd never believe how close it is to Ölüdeniz.'

'To where?' asked Jude.

'A very thoroughly developed seaside resort,' said Carole, pleased to offer more of her guidebook research. 'Only a few miles away, but there you can find everything you'd expect in a tourist centre – water sports, beach umbrellas, English package-holiday people . . .'

Jude grinned. 'So in what way are we not "English package-holiday people"?'

'Well, we aren't here on a package holiday, for a start,' Carole replied righteously. 'We're staying in a private villa. That's entirely different.'

'I see,' said Jude, still amused.

'No,' Carole went on, 'Ölüdeniz is very touristy. Not our sort of place at all. Rather ghastly, I believe.'

'I live in Ölüdeniz,' said Nita.

It could have been an awkward moment. Carole certainly thought it was. But Jude, catching Nita's eye in the rear-view mirror, winked and received an answering grin.

'It's practical,' Nita continued. 'My husband's business is in Ölüdeniz.'

'Ah, now, he teaches scuba diving – is that right? Barney mentioned it.'

'Yes, Jude, he has a school in Ölüdeniz. If you fancy having some lessons, there's a flyer with all the details in the villa.'

'Yes, I think it's probably unlikely, but never say never.' Jude's response to the suggestion was rather more gracious than Carole's had been.

'Right. We actually only live in Ölüdeniz during the summer – you know, the tourist season. In the winter we're in Muğla, which is where Erkan's family comes from.'

'And do you have children?' asked Carole, now feeling ready to pose a personal question.

But the sharpness with which Nita said, 'No,' made her

wish she hadn't. Still, the awkwardness was not allowed to linger, as their guide went on briskly, 'Anyway, Ölüdeniz is a temple of culture and good taste when compared to Hisarönü.'

'Where?'

'It's a village – well, maybe I should say it used to be a village – only a few miles away. Between Kayaköy and Ölüdeniz, and that's really touristy.'

'For tourists from where?' asked Jude.

'Oh, English, definitely English. All the cafés and restaurants do full English breakfasts – and Sunday roasts. Lots of pubs called things like the Rover's Return. And the Dirty Duck, of course, that Donna mentioned. People can spend a fortnight there and never hear anyone speaking anything but English.'

'Oh dear,' said Carole Seddon as her mind clouded with images of tattoos and Union Jack T-shirts. And she had another little niggle of worry about the shorts on Lily's teddy bear.

'It sounds fun,' said Jude. 'We really must go there.'

The Hyundai turned off left fairly soon after the road levelled out at the beginning of the village. The track up which they travelled was just wide enough for one car but, unlike the potholed route they had taken from Fethiye, it was well-paved. The sides of the track were wooded, but here and there were turnings, presumably leading to other villas.

When they emerged from the woods on to a paved forecourt, through black railed gates they saw Morning Glory in all its glory. The central part of the building, rising to three storeys, was made of slabs of old grey stone. That part must have been some existing structure, a granary perhaps, considering its height, but to either side new wings had been sympathetically added. They were constructed mostly of wood and glass, but pillars and rows of stone contrived to make the whole villa look like a single concept. A wooden garage door presumably hid the car that Barney Willingdon had promised them the use of.

Between the gates and the front door, a large swimming pool sparkled in the sunlight. Water trickled continually over its outer edge into a conduit from which it was recycled back into the pool, so that swimmers had the illusion of an infinite vista beyond. Around the pool, loungers lay, attended by palm trees. And any harsh contours of the building were softened by variegated shrubs and potted plants.

Carole and Jude's spirits lifted. Both felt relief from looking at the home where they would spend the next fortnight. All Carole's fears of being overlooked or surrounded by lager louts with tattoos and Union Jack T-shirts vanished in an instant.

Jude let out a low whistle. 'Wow!' she said.

'Pretty damn good, isn't it?' said Nita with almost proprietorial pride. 'Mind you, you're not seeing it quite at its best.'

'Oh?'

'Wait till tomorrow morning.'

'What do you mean?'

'The villa's not called Morning Glory for nothing.' She gestured to the greenery climbing up over the villa's frontage. 'The flowers close up in the afternoon. Tomorrow morning that'll be a riot of blue.'

'Lovely. Can't wait to see it,' said Jude.

'Right, let's get in and show you round.' Nita reached for a zapper from the car's glove compartment and opened the gates remotely. She parked on the paved surface directly in front of the main door. 'Do you want to bring your bags in now or have a look around first?'

Carole's, 'Bring the bags in,' and Jude's, 'Have a look around,' were spoken simultaneously. Jude's counsel won.

As they got out, their guide produced a large ring of keys from the glove compartment. Once again, after the air-conditioned comfort of the car, the direct sunlight felt very fierce.

As Nita unlocked the double wooden doors, she said, 'Obviously, there's air conditioning throughout. Up to you whether you want to have that on or open the doors and windows to get a through breeze.' Then, pushing the doors wide, she stood back. 'See what you think.'

Carole and Jude stepped forward into Morning Glory. They were aware of a large white-painted room, taking up the whole ground floor of the original building. But, before they could take in any more, both were drawn to the words written on the high white wall opposite them:

'YOU ARE NOT WELLCOME HERE. REMEMBER WHAT HAPPNED TO ZOE.'

Trails of red dripped down from some of the letters. They appeared to be written in blood.

Carole Seddon, who never did that kind of thing, screamed.

NINE

T he first thing established was that it wasn't blood. With what Carole thought of as complete disregard for the etiquette of behaviour at what could be a crime scene, Nita had gone straight across to the writing and touched a finger to the residual dampness on the letters. She sniffed the red deposit and announced, 'Paint.'

'Are you sure?' asked Carole in her most businesslike way, trying retrospectively to cover up the appalling lapse of her emotional display.

'Yes.'

'Might it have been done by some locals who resent British ownership of property out here?'

'Very unlikely,' said Nita. 'Almost everyone in Kayaköy is involved in the tourist industry.'

'But the fact that the message is misspelt suggests it was written by someone whose first language isn't English.'

'I wouldn't be so sure of that,' said Nita drily. 'I've dealt with some pretty illiterate English holidaymakers over the years. Anyway, as I was saying, none of the locals would do anything that might harm the tourist industry. And they take a pretty dim view of anyone who *does* harm it. They have fairly effective methods of policing their own community. Any teenager who steps out of line and commits some act of vandalism is treated in such a way that they never do it again. Apart from anything else, the people here really like the British.'

'So who else might have done this?'

'I've no idea.'

'But who,' asked Carole, 'knew we were going to be out here?'

'I don't think this is addressed at you personally,' said Nita, her reassurance not entirely subduing Carole's paranoia. 'Nobody did know you were going to be out here. Your names may be on a form somewhere, but I doubt it. I gather your taking the villa is a private arrangement between you and Barney.'

'Yes, it is.'

'So this—' Nita gestured to the defaced wall – 'is not aimed at you.'

'Who is it aimed at, then?'

The tour guide shrugged. Carole and Jude got the strong impression that she did have an idea who might have desecrated the white interior wall. They received the equally strong impression that she wasn't about to share her suspicions with them.

Nita pulled an iPhone from the pocket of her white trousers. On its dark-blue case was a design of pale-blue fishes.

'And seeing what it says up there,' asked Carole, 'what *did* happen to Zoë?'

But Nita had got through on the phone and was speaking in fluent Turkish. When she finished her call she said, 'I was talking to my husband, Erkan. He will come and tidy up that mess. Now let us continue with our guided tour of the house.'

'I would still like to know,' insisted Carole, 'what happened to Zoë Willingdon!'

'By which I gather Barney hasn't told you?'

'No, he hasn't.'

'Well, I think it's something he should do himself. He'll tell you this evening.'

'This evening?' asked Jude.

'Didn't he tell you? Barney's coming to take the two of you out for dinner tonight.'

'Oh?'

'He'll arrive about seven.'

*   *   *

When they had finished their tour of the villa – and very impressive they'd found it – they came back downstairs to find a wiry, dark man had already started painting over the red letters in the main room. He wore jeans and a plaid shirt with sleeves buttoned at the wrist. The hair which covered his hands and sprouted from his collar beneath the shaving line suggested that his whole body was covered with it.

'This is Erkan, my husband,' said Nita. She spoke without enthusiasm. 'Carole . . . and Jude.'

They shook hands rather formally. 'Welcome to Turkey,' he said in good but heavily accented English. Given the backdrop of words behind him, his greeting seemed slightly ironical.

'Just let me show you the kitchen area,' said Nita. 'I don't know whether you'll be doing much cooking while you're out here?'

'I'd think the odd cup of coffee,' said Jude. 'Otherwise, we'll eat out most of the time.'

'I'm sure we'll have some meals in,' said Carole, predictably enough.

Suddenly, they heard a distant amplified wailing sound filling the Kayaköy valley.

'What on earth's that?' asked Carole.

'It's the *muezzin*,' Nita replied.

'Ah.' Carole recognized the expression from one of her crosswords. 'He's on the minaret, calling the people to prayer?'

'Exactly. Though most of them use loudspeakers these days.'

'So what should we do?'

'What do you mean?'

'Well, I mean, it's a religious thing, isn't it? And one doesn't want to show disrespect to other religions. So should we . . . I don't know . . . stand up?'

'We are standing up,' said Jude.

A puzzled look flashed from Nita to Jude, who shrugged as if to say, '*Sorry, that's what Carole's like.*'

Nita moved towards the fridge. 'You'll find this is pretty well stocked.' She opened the door to demonstrate. '*Extremely* well stocked' might have been more accurate. There was bread, eggs, bacon, salami, cheese, tomatoes, cucumbers, fresh fruit and large water bottles at the bottom. In the shelves of the door stood milk, bottles of wine – red white and rosé – and cans of Efes beer. The white wine, Carole noted, was not Chardonnay. Some kind of Sauvignon Blanc. She thought she probably wouldn't like it.

'We won't starve with that lot,' said Jude.

'No, you should be fine for a day or two. But when you do need to go to the supermarket, there are three in the village. Go to the nearest one on the main street. It's run by Erkan's cousin. Say you're staying at Morning Glory and you'll get extra-good service.'

'Thank you.'

Nita looked at her watch as she closed the fridge door, and then led the way back into the main room. 'I must go. I have to meet some other people from a flight at Dalaman.' She took out of her pocket a red and blue striped lanyard with an ID card on it and slipped it round her neck. 'Into business mode,' she said with a grimace.

'Oh, well, thank you so much for meeting us,' said Jude. 'It's really appreciated.'

'Yes, so kind,' said Carole, unable to stop the words from sounding false and patronizing.

'No problem. Barney reckons he'll be with you about seven.'

'OK, fine.'

'I'm sure I'll see you again during your stay. And you've got my mobile number in case of any emergency—' she grinned sardonically – 'like a blocked toilet.'

'Thank you very much for all you've done,' said Jude.

'No problem. See you later.'

And, without a word to her husband, Nita left Morning Glory. She took Carole and Jude's bags out of the Hyundai and drove off down the steep track. If Erkan was upset by his wife's behaviour, he showed no signs of it. He just continued covering the red letters with white paint.

'Well, I suppose unpacking comes next,' suggested Carole.

'Hm. It's tempting just to grab a bikini and leap into the pool.'

'Well, it may tempt you, but I'm not going to go into the pool until I've unpacked.' Doing anything else would, to Carole, have seemed like having a cake at tea before she'd

had any bread and butter. Besides, there was a potential embar-
rassment ahead if she went swimming. She was rather afraid
her money belt might look a bit silly under her costume. But
then where else could she put it where it'd be safe?

'Talking of money,' she said (which they hadn't been),
'maybe we should put some into your kitty purse?'

'Yes. OK if we both put in, say . . . a couple of hundred
lira?'

'A bit more than that, I'd think.'

'It'll be all right, just for a start. We won't need to stock
up at the supermarket for a few days.'

'But what about dinner tonight, if we're going out?'

'Barney will pay for that.'

'Oh, we can't let him pay. Then we'd feel beholden to him.'

'Barney has so much money that he wouldn't notice a meal
for three in a Turkish restaurant.'

'That's not the point, Jude.'

'I'd have thought it was exactly the point.'

Carole Seddon looked beadily at her neighbour. 'Have you
and Barney ever been lovers?'

'No,' Jude lied.

'Good,' said Carole. 'Otherwise I'd feel that if he pays for
tonight's dinner, we'd be . . . well, living on immoral
earnings.'

To prevent a major lapse into hysterics, Jude said quickly,
'I think I must go and find that bikini.'

True to her word, Jude had only unpacked to the extent of
pulling a bikini out of her bag. Morning Glory was well
equipped with a selection of bright bathing towels, freshly
laundered like all of the house's bedding. Shoeless, she went
downstairs and out to the pool. Casting her towel on to a
lounger, she went to the steps and lowered her considerable
bulk into the water's warm embrace.

From the window of her room, Carole looked down at her
friend splashing idly about and, as she had so many times
before, envied Jude's apparent insouciance. Then she unpacked,
meticulously and very slowly. She felt ill at ease now they
had actually arrived at Morning Glory, embarrassed about

actually putting on her costume. And she also had a sensation of decisions having been taken out of her hands. Their first evening she'd reckoned should be a quiet night in, getting used to the villa. And now Barney Willingdon was dragooning them into going out for dinner. And no doubt paying for it, once again making her feel beholden.

One thing even Carole couldn't fault, though, was the quality of their accommodation. Morning Glory had been beautifully designed, and everything about the building had been done to a very high spec. Barney Willingdon may himself have been something of a rough diamond, but he certainly knew where to find the best architects and interior designers. Or maybe, she wondered, was it – as it had probably been at Chantry House – that Henry had been the one with the 'eye'? Except Morning Glory might well have been built while Barney was still married to Zoë. Anyway, whoever was responsible, they had done a very good job.

The only negative Carole could find in her accommodation was the sign next to the lavatory in her bathroom, which read: 'Please refrain from throwing toilet paper in the toilet. It may lead to imminent blockage. Thank you.' This came as a shock to her. Surely a society that could convert an old building into a villa with such sophistication should be capable of flushing away toilet paper? But she did, nonetheless, obey the notice's injunction.

Carole thought again about the now-covered painted message that had greeted them. And she wondered why her first instinctive thought about it was that she was present at a crime scene – and that the offence had not just been the misdemeanour of defacing a wall. She'd had the distinct feeling that the painted message had been part of some other, greater crime. One that had already been – or maybe was yet to be – committed.

She looked down again to the pool. From the height of her bedroom she could see its 'infinity' feature. The water just seemed to flow off the edge of the world. Jude had spread her towel over a lounger and flopped on to it. Swelling out of the bikini, there was quite a lot of her. And yet Carole knew that if she were on the adjacent lounger – even if she, too, was wearing a bikini (perish the thought) – it was on Jude that any passing male's eyes would linger. She tried, unsuccessfully, not to feel jealous.

Carole Seddon continued making a slow meal of her unpacking.

TEN

D own by the pool, Jude thought idly that she should have brought her trashy novel with her. Or had a look at the stock of trashy novels left by previous guests. It was a fairly predictable selection, mostly in English, but some in German and Dutch. Danielle Steel, Wilbur Smith, Dan Brown and, she'd noticed, two abandoned copies of *Fifty Shades of Grey*.

But going upstairs to fetch a book would be far too much trouble. More importantly, she should have anointed herself with some suntan cream. Though it felt benign, the late afternoon sun retained its potential to burn, and her skin had not had any previous exposure to its beams that year. But again, the journey back into Morning Glory and up the stairs to her room seemed an insuperable challenge. Jude's eyelids drooped and closed.

From the point of view of her skin, it was probably just as well that she was woken after ten minutes of dozing by an English voice saying, 'Just came to introduce myself.'

Disoriented, she looked up at the figure outlined by the descending sun. It took a few seconds and a hand shading her eyes before she could see him distinctly. Revealed was a thin man probably in his sixties with no hair, thin metal-rimmed glasses and a tan so dark that he looked as if he'd been pickled like a walnut. He wore only khaki-coloured shorts and leather sandals, the latter incongruously over thick beige socks.

He held out a hand, which Jude stretched forward to shake. Some women might have been embarrassed sitting there in only a skimpy bikini, but not Jude. Or, at least, not at first.

'My name's Travers Hughes-Swann,' said the newcomer.

'I'm Jude.'

'Nice to meet you.'

'Won't you sit down? Can I get you a drink or something?'

'No, no, don't bother, please. I'm not one of those people who's dependent on their drink. And I never touch alcohol. But I will just sit for a moment.' He perched his bony buttocks on the edge of an adjacent lounger. 'I'm just a neighbour, so I thought I'd be neighbourly and say hello.'

'Oh?'

'I live in the next villa. Called Brighton House. You can't see it through the trees, but it's quite close. Very close, actually.'

'Ah. Well, I'm here with my friend Carole, and we're staying for a fortnight.'

'Yes, I know.'

'Really?'

'No secrets in a place like Kayaköy. Everyone knows everyone else's business. And everyone knows about all the comings and goings to the various villas.'

'Oh.' What he'd said gave Jude a slightly uncomfortable feeling. Morning Glory had seemed so perfectly remote, but clearly the village had eyes and ears. She was also rather aware now that Travers Hughes-Swann had eyes too. And they did seem to be rather fixated on her cleavage.

From her bedroom upstairs, Carole peered out of the window. God, it didn't take long for Jude to meet new people. She slowed down her unpacking even more. She felt she personally had met quite enough new people for one day. She didn't want to go down to the pool and get involved in all that business of introductions and explaining herself.

'Do you live out here permanently?' asked Jude, intuiting from his tan that he probably did.

He confirmed this. 'Yes. After I'd retired I needed to get out of the UK. Place fell apart after they did the dirty on Margaret Thatcher. We stuck it for a few more years under that idiot John Major, but things clearly weren't going to get any better, so we upped sticks and came out here.'

'Do you go back to England much?'

'Not if I can help it, no. Walk along the streets there and you hardly hear an English voice. All speaking Bengali or Somali or something like that. And us paying for their welfare with our taxes. Whole country's gone to the dogs.'

Jude didn't make any comment, but not for the first time she was struck by how perversely racist a lot of expatriates were. One might have thought they lived abroad with a view to inter-mingling, building bridges with the locals, but in her experience that very rarely seemed to be the case. They kept themselves to themselves and nurtured recollections of a home country so perfect as never to have existed. 'When you say "we" . . .?'

'Wife Phyllis. "Her Indoors." Though sadly saying "Her Indoors" these days is all too accurate.'

'Oh?'

'Bedridden, I'm afraid. Has been for years.'

'I'm sorry.'

'Yes. But one gets used to most things,' he said in a matter-of-fact way. 'So Phyllis is "Her Indoors" while I am "Him Outdoors".' His little chuckle suggested he thought this was funny. 'Spend most of my time in the garden. I've landscaped it all myself. Can be tricky working on a slope like this, but I've put a lot of hard work into it. Built some splendid garden features from the local stone, they look really authentic. It's a labour of love, actually; I've been doing it for years. And it looks pretty damn good, let me tell you.'

'I'm sure it does.' Jude looked around. 'This one's not bad either, is it?'

'If you like that kind of thing,' said Travers Hughes-Swann sniffily. 'All done by paid gardeners, though. Looks a bit sanitized for my taste.'

'Oh.'

'Still, that's the way Barney does everything, isn't it? Or, rather, doesn't do anything. Doesn't do anything hands-on, anyway. Pays people to come and sort things out for him.'

'Surely, that's a good thing, though, isn't it? So long as he selects the right people to do the jobs.'

'Yes, I suppose so,' her visitor conceded. 'If you can afford it. Which he certainly can.' There was undisguised envy in his voice.

'Did Barney actually build your villa too?'

'No, ours has been here much longer. Converted farm building. Much more authentic than this.' He gestured contemptuously to the splendour of Morning Glory. 'Or any of the others that Barney's built. He's got more concern for the home comforts of middle-class English people than he has for preserving the genuine flavour of Turkish tradition.'

Jude thought that the villa seemed to do a pretty good job of mixing ancient and modern, but didn't make any comment. She did feel mildly interested though, to see, at some point, how Brighton House had preserved tradition more faithfully. At some point – but that wasn't a point of any great urgency. She couldn't see herself exactly seeking out Travers Hughes-Swann's company over the next two weeks.

By now, though, he did seem dangerously ensconced on the edge of his lounger, gazing fixedly at her cleavage, and she was beginning to wonder how she was going to get rid of him. 'I must go in soon,' she said. 'Mustn't have too much sun on my first day. And I haven't even started unpacking.'

'Right.' He sounded disappointed by the news. 'Well, if there's anything you and your friend Carole need to know, anything we can help you with, just say the word. We'll be glad to help – well, that is, I'll be glad to help. I'm afraid Phyllis can't even help herself these days. You can't miss our place. We're first left down the track. Brighton House, as I said.'

'Thank you. Did you call it that because you used to live in Brighton?'

He looked puzzled by the suggestion. 'Good Lord, no. Full of poofs, Brighton.' For a moment he seemed aware of some lapse in political correctness. 'Or what do they like to be called now – gays? God, and now you've got same-sex marriages in the UK, haven't you? I'm not religious, but I think that's really offensive, disgusting to normal people like me. You know, there is a lot to be said for living in a Muslim country.'

'But you haven't converted to Islam?'

'God, no. I'm not barmy.' Reluctantly, he stood up. 'As I say, anything you need, just drop in.'

'Thank you so much.' Jude lifted herself out of her lounger

and, with some relief, wrapped the towel around her ample curves. 'Oh, just one thing, Travers . . .'

'Hm?'

'Have you known Barney Willingdon a long time?'

'Oh yes. Met him when he first started thinking of building out here. Must be fifteen years ago, at least. I've watched him build every one of his villas, watched his property empire expand and expand.'

'Did you ever meet his first wife?'

'Zoë? God, yes.'

'I gather she died . . .?'

'Yes, far too young. Pretty little thing.'

'And do you know how she died?'

'Yes,' said Travers Hughes-Swann. 'Scuba-diving accident.'

Cin Bal was an altogether different experience in eating, particularly if you had sampled as little foreign cuisine as Carole Seddon had. For her, going to a Chinese or Indian in Fedborough verged on the exotic.

The low stone-built restaurant was at the centre of a huge area set under trees in the middle of the Kayaköy valley. While the building may have been used during the colder seasons, when the weather improved everyone sat outside. Tables spread in every direction, but there was no sense of crush. Overhead vines were trained to make a kind of awning. Low circles of cemented stones protected the many trees. There was a high noise-level from the many large parties of Turkish families enjoying their evening. And everything was pervaded by the smells of burning charcoal and barbecuing meat.

Barney Willingdon was clearly a regular at Cin Bal. As soon as he had left his white Range Rover in the car park, people were calling out greetings to him, and the nearer they got to the restaurant building the more he seemed to know. Jude grinned amiably at any who came close, while Carole kept her eyes straight ahead. The whole set-up felt very alien to her and, whatever might be offered from the menu, she was determined she would not have a kebab. (She had her Imodium safely to hand in her bag.)

At the entrance to the building stood a tall man in black shirt and trousers who clearly had some kind of official function. 'Good evening, Mr Willingdon,' he said in heavily accented English. 'Would you like to find a table before you . . .?'

'No, I'll have my usual one.'

'Very good, Mr Willingdon.'

'We'll go straight through to choose our food.'

'Very good.'

'But could you set up some drinks for us?'

'Of course.'

'I'll have an Efes beer to start with, then probably move on to the red wine. Jude, Carole, what are you drinking?'

'Tend to prefer white,' said Jude.

'Chardonnay, if that's convenient,' said Carole clumsily.

'Have the Chardonnay if you want to, by all means,' said Barney, 'but if you'll be advised by me, try the Sauvignon Blanc. There's a local one they do here which is absolutely delicious.'

'Well, I'm not sure that I—'

But Carole was immediately cut off by Jude's assertion that they'd love to try the Sauvignon Blanc.

Inside the restaurant building were rows of glass-fronted refrigerated display cabinets. In the first ones they came to were large trays full of starters – an infinite array of dips, salads, stuffed vegetables, shellfish, octopus, sausages and pastries. A waiter with a notepad at the ready hovered to take their order. 'Just choose what you like,' said Barney.

'Is that hummus?' asked Carole tentatively. Hummus she had heard of. Hummus could be bought in Waitrose and Sainsbury's. (It could even be bought in the budget supermarket Lidl, though of course Carole Seddon didn't know that.)

'Yes,' Barney replied.

'Well, I think I'll have some of that.'

'And what else?'

'That'll be plenty, thank you.'

Barney thought they might need a few more starters, and Jude was, unsurprisingly, more adventurous than her friend. She went for octopus salad, stuffed courgette flowers and an aubergine dip.

'Have some *börek* too,' said Barney. He pointed to some triangular envelopes of pastry. 'Filled with cheese and herbs. They'll be served hot – very good.'

'But don't you think we've got enough?' suggested Carole.

'No,' said Barney and, with a few words in Turkish to the waiter, he moved along to the next row of display cabinets. This was the meat. As well as trays of steaks, livers, cutlets and other joints, above them hung down whole split carcasses of beef and lamb. 'We'll get some of each,' said Barney. 'And a bit of chicken.'

'How will it be cooked?' asked Carole cautiously, fearful that she would soon hear the word 'kebab'.

'However you want.'

'Sorry? What do you mean?'

'We do the cooking ourselves.'

And that was how it happened. They arrived at their table to find their drinks ready for them. A waiter poured Barney's Efes beer into a frosted glass, then unscrewed the lid of the white wine and, without any tasting ritual, charged glasses for the two women.

Jude took an instant sip. They'd had drinks with Barney on the terrace of Morning Glory, but the evening heat made her still thirsty. 'Ooh,' she said as she took the glass away from her lips, 'that's gorgeous.'

'Told you it would be,' said Barney.

Carole took a tentative sip. She didn't make any comment, though she, too, thought it was gorgeous. But, as so often with Carole Seddon, a positive feeling was very quickly replaced by a negative one. Would she be betraying her long allegiance to Chilean Chardonnay? And she'd got seven bottles left in a case back at High Tor. It'd be a terrible waste if those didn't get drunk.

A man, whose hangdog demeanour suggested a lowly position in the Cin Bal hierarchy, came towards them pushing a trolley. It took a moment for the two women to realize that the open metal box he carried was full of burning charcoal. Their own personal barbecue, which the man affixed to the side of their table. Soon after that their starters arrived, and in due course the cuts of meat they had ordered. These were covered with upturned plates, presumably to keep off the flies. Though, in fact, there seemed to be very few flies around, maybe kept away by the charcoal smoke.

As Barney had said, it was completely up to them how they cooked their meal. The process couldn't have been more hands-on. Those who wanted their meat pink and bloody could have it pink and bloody; and those who wanted it charred to a crisp could char it to a crisp personally.

But with the salads and the wine it tasted wonderful. All of them at the table mellowed and relaxed. Even Carole Seddon began to feel that going away on holiday to Turkey had been rather a good idea. Fethering was all very well in its way, but it was good to be reminded that a world existed outside the village. Perhaps there were more foreign destinations that she should sample.

Also, the quality of the Sauvignon Blanc made her consider yet again the ultimate sacrifice. The next time she went to the Crown and Anchor in Fethering, she might order something other than Chilean Chardonnay. How on earth would Ted Crisp react to such a seismic change?

Throughout the meal, Barney was constantly greeted by other friends or business associates. Clearly, he was a popular man around Kayaköy. Or maybe his popularity was based on more mercenary motives. His developments had brought a lot of work to the local builders and craftsmen (who were all cousins, anyway). The holidaymakers who stayed in his villas also made their contribution to the local economy.

And Barney enjoyed his local celebrity. He cheerily shook hands with all the men who approached him and greeted the women with lavish hugs and kisses. Or, at least, that's what he did with the women dressed in western clothes. He did not hug and kiss the ones in traditional dress; he knew the local protocols.

When Barney had arrived earlier in the evening at Morning Glory, no reference had been made to the message in red that had confronted the visitors earlier. They'd had drinks by the pool, so he hadn't actually entered the villa and seen the evidence of the still-wet white paint. But Jude felt the subject ought to be raised, so she raised it.

'Yes, I heard about that,' said Barney. He didn't say who he'd heard it from, but that didn't seem important to Jude. She remembered Travers Hughes-Swann telling her that there were 'no secrets in a place like Kayaköy'. The bush telegraph of brothers and cousins had no doubt been extremely efficient.

'I'm sorry,' Barney went on. 'Not the greeting I would have wished for you. And, incidentally, it wasn't aimed at you personally.'

'Then who was it aimed at?' asked Carole.

'Just the Brits generally.' There was an evasiveness in his eye which Jude recognized from some of the less happy moments in their long ago relationship.

'But who would have done that? Nita told us most of the locals are somehow involved in the tourist industry and wouldn't dream of doing anything to disrupt it.'

'Yes, but there's always an element. There's a bunch of ultra-nationalist kids in Fethiye who resent us Brits profiting from their tourist trade.'

Jude reckoned he was lying, just making up an explanation so that they could move on to another subject of conversation. 'Are you saying it was aimed at you, then?' she persisted.

'Probably. You can't do the kind of work I do out here without putting a few backs up.' He looked at their glasses. 'I think we're going to need another bottle of Sauvignon Blanc.'

'Oh no,' came the knee-jerk reaction from Carole.

'Come on,' said Barney. 'I'm more than halfway down my bottle of red and feeling no pain. Have the second bottle.'

'Well . . .' said Carole.

'Let's go for it,' said Jude. 'After all, we are on holiday.'

ELEVEN

B ecause of the effusiveness Barney had demonstrated towards other women that evening, it was quite striking that when Nita emerged through the trees to approach their table he didn't rise from his seat and offer her either a hug or a kiss. Just said a casual, 'Hi.'

Round her neck hung the red and blue lanyard with identity card attached. She didn't wear a polo shirt with a company logo on it, but presumably the card identified her for professional purposes. It also suggested she was either still working or had just finished.

'Got your other person from the airport?' asked Jude.

'Yes, all done and safely delivered to their villa. I get the impression they're going to be high maintenance, though.'

'Oh?'

'Already had two calls from them on the mobile. How do they get hot water from the shower, and can they set up the telly to receive Sky Sports? Needless to say, there are detailed instructions for dealing with both problems in their welcome pack. Soon, I'm sure, I'll get the call about the blocked toilet. I think I'll earn my money with that lot.'

'They've gone into Sunbeam Cottage,' said Barney, as a statement rather than a question.

'Right.'

Belatedly, Barney remembered his manners. 'Won't you sit down and have a drink?'

'No, still got a couple of things to sort out. Got to take a busload of punters who've come from Kidderminster to Pinara tomorrow.'

Carole's ears pricked up. 'That's where there are some Lycian tombs, isn't it?'

'Yes. And temples, and an amphitheatre.'

'I definitely want to go there while I'm here. I read about it in my guidebook. It sounds fascinating, with all those tombs carved out of the rock face. Do you fancy going tomorrow, Jude?'

'I don't fancy going anywhere tomorrow that is more than three metres from the pool at Morning Glory.'

'Oh. Well.' Carole turned back to Nita. 'Pinara's supposed to be very impressive, isn't it?'

'It is for the first couple of hundred times you see it, yes. After that, everything palls a bit.'

'I'm sure it does,' said Jude.

'But that's the job – not the one that I would have chosen, but the one that's chosen me.' Nita looked down at her ID card and sighed. 'So that's the job I do.'

Jude was aware that Nita was not talking to them as she would to her normal punters. She was dropping her professional guard and letting her underlying cynicism show. She thought of them not so much as holidaymakers but as friends of Barney Willingdon. She didn't have to keep up any facade with them.

'Anyway . . .' Nita snapped herself out of introspection. 'I must go, brush up my notes on Pinara. See you soon, I'm sure.' She hovered on the edge of departure. 'Oh, Barney, just wondering whether you might be going for a nightcap at the Scorpion tonight . . .?'

'No, I'll just be seeing Carole and Jude back to Morning Glory.'

'And which of the villas are you staying in?'

'I haven't decided yet,' said Barney Willingdon.

Nita was not the kind of woman to give away her emotions, but she flinched at his words. 'Right,' she said, 'I'll go and get ready for Pinara.'

Jude was trying to work out the subtext of their brief exchange. Surely, Nita had been trying to get together alone with Barney, but he had put an end to such an idea with considerable harshness. She hoped to God he wasn't clearing the decks of other women because he thought he was going to make some progress with her.

But such speculation was interrupted by the sudden appearance at their table of a swarthy middle-aged man in grubby T-shirt and jeans, brandishing a kitchen knife.

'You dare come out here!' he shouted in heavily accented English. 'You dare to sit here calmly in Cin Bal as if you are the king of everything!'

His words were clearly addressed to Barney, who instantly recognized his assailant. 'Kemal,' he said, 'calm down.'

Jude's ears pricked up. This must be the swindled partner of Barney whom Fergus McNally had mentioned in the Crown and Anchor.

'Violence won't do you any good,' said Barney.

'No? It will do me a lot of good – to hurt the man who has ruined my life, who took away my business—'

'I didn't take away your business. That was going belly-up long before I got involved.'

'No, you took it away. You took away my livelihood. To hurt the man who did this will give me much satisfaction!' And he made a stabbing motion with the knife towards Barney.

He missed by a long way, and instantly Carole and Jude realized that the man was very drunk. His movements were unsteady and his eyes glazed. By now, the commotion had attracted attention from the neighbouring tables and black-dressed waiters were moving towards the source of the trouble. Barney had stood up to get out of the range of Kemal's weapon.

The attacker made another swinging slash with his knife, but the force of it overbalanced him, and he stumbled on to the dusty ground. From there, two of the waiters disarmed and picked him up, efficiently putting him into an armlock.

The tall, dark-clad man who had greeted Barney at the entrance to the restaurant moved forward, and the two of them had a muttered conversation in Turkish. The man seemed to be trying to persuade Barney of something – Carole thought she heard a word like 'police' – but the Englishman was having none of it.

Eventually, Barney won his way and, on instructions from their superior, the two waiters frogmarched the bleary Kemal through the trees towards the complex's entrance, where presumably he would be thrown off the premises. After a couple more words with the tall man, Barney Willingdon resumed his seat and topped up his glass of red wine. 'Sorry about that,' he said, in a manner that was far too urbane for the circumstances.

'Have they called the police?' asked Carole.

'No.'

'Why ever not? That man attacked you with a knife. He should be charged with attempted murder.'

'That's taking the incident far too seriously. He's drunk, that's all.'

'There are plenty of victims who've been murdered by somebody who was drunk.'

'I'm sure there are. But, as you can see, I'm not one of them. Let's talk about something else . . . like how you're going to spend your fortnight in the lovely village of Kayaköy.'

After the scene they'd just witnessed, Jude was beginning to wonder how lovely the village of Kayaköy actually was. Then, remembering what she'd heard from Fergus McNally, she asked, 'Did that man Kemal use to be a business partner of yours, Barney?'

He looked annoyed that she had made the connection, and a little confused as to how she might have made it, but conceded that Kemal and he had been in business together. 'But we fell out over the definition of hard work. Kemal thought all he had to contribute to our mutual projects was a Turkish name on the letterhead. It didn't occur to him that he was actually expected to get his hands dirty.'

'I see,' said Jude, thinking that Fergus McNally – and indeed Kemal himself – might have described the situation differently.

When they got back to Morning Glory, Carole, who had had more wine than she was used to, said she would turn in straight away. 'You know, having had such an early start this morning and what with the time difference and everything.'

Jude thought it would be cruel to point out that the time difference worked the other way and that she'd gained a couple of hours rather than lost them. Back in Fethering it was only nine o'clock in the evening.

'Well, goodnight, Carole,' said Barney. 'Nita did show you how the air conditioning worked, didn't she?'

'Oh yes. But I won't be using it.' To Carole's mind, air conditioning was an entirely unnecessary form of pampering. She'd been brought up in an English home where no mechanical aids were allowed to interfere with the regular sequence of the seasons. In the winter you got cold, in the summer you got hot.

Jude was sorry that Carole had retired for the night because that left her alone with Barney and, after the phone call she'd had from him on the Friday, she anticipated a slightly awkward encounter.

And that's what it proved to be. In spite of having put away a large Efes and the full bottle of red wine, Barney accepted her half-hearted offer of another drink. Reluctantly, she produced her duty-free bottle of Laphroaig and took it, along with two glasses, out to the loungers by the pool. It was a beautiful evening, still pleasantly warm, a tapestry of bright stars spread out over the cloudless sky. Far too romantic, thought Jude as she filled the glasses.

Any hopes she'd nurtured that Barney might have forgotten or felt embarrassed about their recent phone call were quickly crushed.

'Jude,' he murmured, 'I meant what I said on Friday.'

'And I meant what *I* said on Friday. I'm not in the business of rekindling old embers with married men.'

'You're not telling me you've never had a relationship with a married man?'

'No,' Jude replied honestly. 'I am not telling you that. But I do exercise my own judgement in the selection of those married men. And as I said when we spoke on the phone last week, I am not about to succumb to your blandishments.'

'Blimey, have you just swallowed a dictionary?'

'I think you know what I mean, Barney.'

'Yes, I do. Or, at least, I know what you think you mean, Jude.' He moved forward on his lounger and put a hand firmly on her knee. 'But there still is something between us, Jude. Emotion that powerful doesn't just go away.'

She didn't remove his hand. To do so would have felt too clumsy, too teenage, as though going through the motions of a bedroom farce. 'Barney, you're talking a very long time ago.

I am not currently looking for any kind of emotional entangle-
ment. And if I were, I'm afraid you aren't the person I would
be entangling with.' That removed the hand on her knee more
effectively than a slap would have done. 'I come back to the
same point, Barney. You're married.'

'Yes, but I'm in a marriage that's not working.'

'That's not my problem. I recommend you find out which
bit of the marriage is not working and sort it out.'

'I can tell you the bit of it that's not working. The sex.'

'Ah. Well, you must—'

'It's stopped. There just isn't any. Henry's completely lost
interest.'

'Then that's something you must work out between the two
of you. It's nothing to do with me.'

'But it could be something to do with you, Jude. When I
think back to the sex you and I used to enjoy together! It was
just so good, so adventurous, so uncomplicated.'

'*We* were uncomplicated back then, Barney. Let's keep that
whole episode as a pleasant memory. It's not going to happen
again. And if it did, I can guarantee that it wouldn't be the
same. You can't go down the same road twice.'

'How do you know that?'

'Just take my word for it.'

'But, Jude . . .' His voice was low, teasing, sexy.

Again, no slap. But Jude found another, equally effective
method of changing Barney's priorities. 'Incidentally,' she said,
'I now know how your first wife died.'

Jude felt uncomfortable as she lay uncovered on the crisp
white sheets of her bed, waiting to feel the benefit of the air
conditioning. (She did not share Carole's inhibitions about
using it.) She felt hot, but the main cause of her discomfort
was not the ambient temperature, but the conversation she'd
had with Barney. Why wouldn't he just take no for an answer?
If he kept up his current behaviour, he would spoil the two
weeks of baggage-free relaxation that Jude had been
planning.

She tried to clear her mind, but her thoughts kept coming
back to the same subject: Barney Willingdon. Not in a romantic

way. Though she could still recognize his attractions, Jude genuinely had no intentions of getting embroiled there again. But she was worried about Barney's moral values. She couldn't forget Fergus McNally's long diatribe against his former partner. And the fumbled attack by Kemal in Cin Bal was troubling too.

There was also Barney's conversation at the restaurant with Nita. That had displayed qualities of a stand-off. The tour guide had deliberately sought him out and then asked if he was going for a nightcap at the Scorpion (presumably one of the village's many bars). To Jude, that question had sounded like an encoded message. She had a feeling that in the past 'a nightcap at the Scorpion' had preceded a sexual encounter between the two. His turning down the offer had been a slap in the face for Nita.

And when Barney had refused even to tell Nita which villa he was spending the night in, the act of rejection was complete. He had made it clear to Nita that any liaison between the two of them had come to an end. Jude hoped to God that wasn't because he planned for her to take Nita's place.

As the room cooled down she drifted off into troubled sleep.

TWELVE

Carole Seddon had trained her body to wake up without the assistance of an alarm clock at half past six every morning. Winter, summer, whenever, she liked to be out on Fethering Beach walking Gulliver before seven o'clock.

So after an interrupted, sweaty night (she should have switched on the air conditioning), Carole was rather disoriented when she woke at six thirty (or, rather, eight thirty in Turkish time). Her first thought, to her surprise, was of Gulliver, and she had a momentary pang, visualizing him in his unfamiliar kennels. She saw that look of pained reproach that only he could do so well. And the unspoken reprimand: *'People like you shouldn't be allowed to own dogs.'*

But then the broad stripe of bright sunlight across her bed brought her back to current reality. Of course, she was in Morning Glory, facing her first full day of holiday. It was a prospect that rather daunted her. Carole felt extremely restless. If a fortnight in Turkey was supposed to be helping her to untwitch, the process certainly hadn't yet started.

And she was already worried about how Jude would want to spend the day. The two of them were, after all, on holiday together. But did that mean they should both follow the same agenda and do everything together? It was so long since Carole Seddon had spent any length of time with another person that such questions troubled her. And although she and Jude were neighbours, there were still many things they didn't know about each other.

After opening all of the bedroom's windows, Carole looked in the cupboard where she had neatly hung and laid out her clothes. Her Burberry was on a hanger in the furthest recesses, and she already knew that it would stay there until she packed to return to England. She felt an idiot for having brought it. The garment looked as reproachful as her image of Gulliver.

For a moment, she lingered over the new beige shorts. If she had felt confident of spending the whole day at Morning Glory undisturbed by visitors, she might have put them on and begun the process of laying down a tan. But the experience of the previous day had warned her that the villa seemed to be open house to anyone who happened to be passing. Travers Hughes-Swann might appear again, so could Nita or Erkan. And, as the owner, Barney Willingdon seemed to come and go as he felt like it. Though Carole didn't mind Jude witnessing the sight, she didn't want any of the others to see her legs. (It should be mentioned that there was nothing wrong with Carole Seddon's legs. Except for the visible trace of a blue vein at the back of each knee, they were unblemished. In fact, they were rather good legs. But Carole herself could never see them that way, and she kept them covered from one year's end to the next.)

So she reverted to her trusty navy-blue trousers. And a very clean, very white T-shirt. She hoped nobody would notice the bulk of her money-belt underneath. As an act of considerable daring, she put leather flip-flops on her feet. Then she went down to the kitchen and opened the doors giving out on to the poolside area.

There was no sign of Jude. Having overheard much of the poolside conversation of the night before, Carole wondered whether her friend was actually even in Morning Glory or whether she'd succumbed to Barney's blandishments and gone off with him. Knowing Jude's track record, Carole wouldn't have put it past her.

There was instant coffee in a kitchen cupboard, so she put the kettle on. Then she inspected the contents of the fridge and decided that she'd have more or less the same breakfast as she would have done in Fethering – toast. She located a bread knife, cut two slices from the rather dry loaf and placed them in the toaster. She found butter and a choice of spreads. Frank Cooper's Original Oxford Marmalade, Marmite, local honey and what she deduced from the picture on the label was cherry jam.

Her guidebook reading had told her that the cherries in Turkey were particularly good, so she boldly went for the jam. Then she sat at the kitchen table and ate her breakfast, wishing she had a copy of *The Times* to concentrate on. Carole Seddon didn't like being at a loose end when she was eating on her own. She knew it was now possible, for an outlay of money, to get newspapers online, but she hadn't worked out how to do it yet. So she'd have to survive the fortnight with no daily paper and just her book of collected crosswords.

As she munched her toast – the cherry jam was excellent – she tried to assess how her stomach felt. She hadn't had much of the Turkish diet yet, but what they had eaten at Cin Bal had been getting very close to a kebab. And she was ready to rush to the Imodium packet if she did feel squittery. But Carole was forced to admit to herself with some surprise that she did actually feel fine.

She washed up her breakfast things with punctilious efficiency and then went upstairs to get *The Rough Guide to Turkey*. Though she had read through the entry about Kayaköy many times, she wanted to have another look at it. And also Pinara. Nita's mention of the site the night before had aroused her interest, and Carole thought it might be a good place to visit in a few days' time.

But the *Rough Guide* did not hold her attention for long. Carole was extremely unrelaxed. She felt she ought to be doing something. But then she always thought she should be doing something. She looked around to see if the kitchen needed cleaning, but Barney Willingdon's staff had left it so immaculate that even she couldn't find fault. And Erkan's overpainting had efficiently erased all traces of the unwelcoming message that had greeted them.

She went upstairs again to collect her book of *Times* crosswords and sat back at the kitchen table, trying to focus her mind on one of them. But her concentration wasn't good, and the nagging knowledge that all the answers were temptingly available at the back of the book meant it didn't feel like she was doing a proper crossword.

She had been there for nearly an hour, not getting on well with the clues and constantly tempted to check the answers, when she heard some movement from upstairs. Carole expected that the sound of the toilet flushing would be followed by the noise of a shower, but it wasn't. Instead, a bleary-looking Jude, dressed in a red bikini even more minimal than the previous day's, appeared at the top of the stairs.

'Good morning, Carole,' she said. 'Haven't you been out yet?'

'No, I've been busy here. Having breakfast and what-have-you.' Though she'd finished her breakfast an hour before.

'Well, come on out. I could see a bit of it from my bedroom window, but you'll only get the full effect from out the front.'

'The full effect of what?'

'Come and see.' Jude took her friend by the hand and pulled her out to the poolside. Then she turned them both round so that they were looking at the front of the villa. They could see exactly why it was called Morning Glory. Delicate blue flowers tumbled down in profusion over the frontage.

'Best time of the day to see them,' said Jude.

'Yes, I can understand that.' Then Carole asked urgently, 'And what are your plans for the day?'

'Plans?' echoed Jude, with some level of incredulity in her voice. 'I haven't got plans. I've only just woken up.'

'Well, presumably you'll have breakfast first and then—'

'No, I was considering having a splosh in the pool first, then having a shower and possibly thinking about breakfast after that.'

'Oh,' said Carole. Jude's attitude seemed far too lackadaisical for her taste. 'But don't we need to do some shopping at some point . . .?'

'At some point, yes. But this isn't that point. The fridge is still very well stocked. We'll get round to it in time.'

Again the reply was far too unstructured. Carole couldn't help saying, 'I've already been up for an hour and a half.'

'Good for you.' Jude looked puzzled. 'And this is really the first time you've been out of doors?'

'Yes.' Jude shook her head in mild bewilderment as her friend went on: 'So . . . do you have any plans for the day or not?'

'No.' Jude shook her head firmly, setting ripples going through her unbrushed blonde hair.

'Planning to stay here?'

'I should think so. Still too knackered to think of going anywhere else.'

'What about meals?'

'Probably stagger out somewhere in the evening. Make do with what we've got here at lunchtime.'

'Are you sure?' asked Carole.

'No, I'm not sure at all. May go out somewhere to eat at lunchtime too. See how we feel.'

'Well, what I feel is that I should be doing something.'

'Fine. You can do something. I can do nothing.'

'Separately?'

'Yes, why not? Where do you want to go?'

Carole hadn't really made any plans, but she didn't want Jude to realize that, so she found herself replying, 'I quite fancy going to Pinara.'

'Right.'

'But I don't want to go there on my own if it's somewhere you want to go; we should maybe wait for another day when we can go together.'

'What is there at Pinara?' asked Jude lazily.

'Well, there's a Higher and Lower Acropolis, and there's a Royal Tomb and an Amphitheatre.'

'Hm. You've yet to offer me something more attractive than my trashy book on a lounger by the pool.'

'I see.' Carole couldn't keep the note of reproof out of her voice.

'Look, in a few days I'm sure I'll feel up to going out on excursions, but at the moment all I want to do is chill out.'

Carole wished Jude wouldn't use expressions like that. 'Very well,' she found herself saying. 'Today I will go to Pinara on my own.'

'That's cool.'

Carole wished Jude wouldn't use expressions like that either.

Having blackmailed herself into saying that she was going to Pinara, there was no way now that she couldn't go there. The idea of driving an unfamiliar car on unfamiliar roads among unfamiliar people frankly terrified her, but she tried not to let Jude see her fear. This did not prove too difficult because her friend seemed only to be interested in slopping about in the pool or flopping about on her lounger. And by the time Carole left, Jude had shown no signs of getting herself any breakfast.

Packing for the trip to Pinara had taken quite a while. Carole wanted to be sure that she'd got everything she might need for her excursion into a foreign country. She took her passport and driving licence, along with the *Rough Guide* and her map of the Turkish coast. She checked that her money belt was invisible under the waistline of her trousers and that she had some lira available in her pocket for minor purchases. She packed a small sponge bag with Factor Fifty suntan cream, mosquito repellent, Anthisan bite and sting cream, sticking plasters, and, of course, Imodium.

She changed her shoes to the sensible ones she had been wearing for the previous day's flight. She didn't think it was safe to drive in flip-flops.

With regard to rations, she wasn't planning to face eating on her own in any Turkish restaurants, but intended to stop at the Kayaköy supermarket Nita had recommended to stock up with bread, tomatoes and maybe some salami. She tried to remember the handy Turkish phrases she had learned for use on shopping trips.

With her bag packed, Carole went down and opened the garage doors, trying to look as if this was the kind of thing she did every day. The car was a white Fiat Bravo, a five-door hatchback that looked as though it was brand new. Jude floated on her back in the pool, unaware, as her friend carefully checked the controls of the car, which was, of course, right-hand drive.

After sufficient familiarization, Carole dared to move the car out of the garage at the top of the track which led down to the village. At the poolside she opened the window and called out, 'Jude!'

A couple of strokes and her friend was beside her, chubby arms supporting her on the non-infinity edge of the pool. 'I'm going to the supermarket,' said Carole, 'but I won't get any stuff for the house because it'll have to sit in the car all day.'

'Fine,' said Jude. 'We can go down later – not that there's really much we need . . . that is, assuming we eat out this evening.'

'Oh, do you think we should? I mean, we did eat out last night. We could easily cook for ourselves.'

'Well, we can decide that later.' Jude was determined that while they were in Kayaköy they would eat out for every meal except breakfast, but there was no point in causing ructions with Carole by telling her that at this early stage of the holiday. 'Enjoy your day,' she said. 'I know I'll enjoy mine.'

'Yes, well, I should think I'd be back round—'

'Whenever,' said Jude, another expression Carole wished she wouldn't use.

Her excursion to the Kayaköy supermarket was not as daunting as she feared it might be. For a start, the word 'supermarket' was a little grand for what it actually was. Given its dimensions, 'corner shop' might have been nearer the mark.

Carefully, Carole parked opposite on the right-hand side. (She was afraid that if she parked it on the left she might instinctively start driving on that side when she returned.) Then

as she crossed to the shop she found herself nervously prac-
tising saying 'hello' ('mare-ha-ba') and was already confused
about which 'goodbye' was the one to be said by the person
leaving a place, as opposed to the one staying.

But the minute she entered the supermarket such fears
became academic because the chubby man behind the till said
in perfect English, 'Good morning to you. You are very
welcome to Kayaköy. And I hope you are finding it is comfortable in Morning Glory.'

'Oh. Yes. Thank you very much. It's delightful.'

Carole got her supplies for the day and a large bottle of
water from the fridge. Then, having felt the direct heat of the
sun just during the short walk from the car, she also bought
a straw hat.

She reckoned from her map that she had to go through Fethiye
to get to Pinara. That reassured her because the tank was only
half-full of fuel and she thought she should fill up before going
out into the Turkish wilderness. She was sure that Fethiye
would have petrol stations, but not so convinced there'd be
many on the minor roads.

She drove the Fiat with incredible caution over the zigzag
track out of the village, only once getting out of first gear.
Locals who knew the road better hooted at her and swept past
on the few parts where there were passing places. In spite of
the car's very efficient air conditioning, Carole found herself
sweating with the stress.

Though Fethiye's traffic could be confusing to a newcomer,
she had studied the map assiduously before leaving Morning
Glory and managed pretty well. The traffic was heavy, but for
her that was almost a bonus, as it gave her more time to read
the direction signs.

Only one strange thing happened. As she was driving along
the seaside road out of the town, Carole saw a man and a
woman get out of a silver Volvo 4 × 4.

The woman was Henry Willingdon.

Carole had never seen the man before, but had Jude been
in the car, she would have identified him as Fergus McNally.

THIRTEEN

J ude was, in fact, having the beginnings of a perfect holiday day at Morning Glory. She had sploshed around idly in the pool for some time, then lazed on a lounger and let the already scorching sun dry her off. Then she'd had a leisurely shower and sensibly anointed herself with Factor Fifteen before putting on a dry bikini and wrapping a diaphanous drape around her ample body.

Breakfast by the pool had consisted of a nectarine chopped up in yogurt, sprinkled with honey. Then more honey on bread and butter. She'd also found in the fridge door a carton of a Turkish favourite, sour cherry juice, which tasted wonderful.

As for plans for the day, she had none. Whatever Carole had said, Jude felt sure that going out to eat in the evening would be part of it, and a visit to the supermarket might have to be fitted in at some point. But there was no pressure to . work out a timescale for either excursion.

She was glad that Carole had gone out for the day. Not from any lack of affection; it was just that Jude recognized the differences in their personalities. Her own method of untwitching involved running her system down to a state of almost complete torpor and then letting her energy rebuild itself. In two or three days she'd be up to thinking about active sightseeing.

Carole, she knew, worked in exactly the opposite way. The tensions within her demanded constant activity. Even though Jude had been aware of the ill-disguised trepidation with which her friend had set off in the Fiat, going to Pinara was an essential part of her holiday acclimatization. After a few days of busily doing things, Carole would, Jude reckoned, be sufficiently relaxed even to spend a few hours on a lounger by the pool.

And by the end of the fortnight it might even be a case of

Jude suggesting excursions and Carole preferring to loll around at Morning Glory.

Jude's poolside idyll was interrupted by a voice saying, 'Hello again.'

She shaded her eyes against the sun to see the unwelcome outline of Travers Hughes-Swann. Instinctively, she felt glad that she still had the wrap on. Thin though it was, it afforded some protection from his prying eyes.

'Oh, good morning,' she said, fearful that his appearance was going to become a daily occurrence. And also mentally rescheduling the urgency of her trip to the supermarket. It was the only excuse she had, should she need to get away from his cloying presence.

'Just came to check you'd settled in all right.'

'Very well indeed, as you see.'

'Sleep well?'

'Like the proverbial log. And will probably fit in a few more hours in the course of the day.'

'Very good, very good. That's what a holiday's for, isn't it?

'Exactly.'

'Just lazing around on your own, with no interruptions.'

'That's what I like, yes,' said Jude, not daring to put quite as much edge into the words as she wanted to.

'Well, I'm sure you've earned a break. What is it you do?'

'I'm a healer.'

'Oh.' That was a conversation-stopper for Travers. He appeared to have no supplementary questions on the subject of healing. Instead he went on, 'I think doing nothing on holiday is entirely legitimate.'

'Good,' said Jude, not feeling any need to have her plans validated by the likes of Travers Hughes-Swann.

'What gets up my nose is people who do nothing and haven't earned the right to do nothing. Benefit scroungers, layabouts, a lot of them immigrants, you know.'

Before he could get up a full head of fascist steam, Jude said, 'Well, we don't have to worry about that kind of thing out in a beautiful place like this, do we?'

Her words had the desired effect of stopping his diatribe before he had really got into it. Travers Hughes-Swann moved his tortoise head around to take in the whole villa. 'I haven't met your friend yet.'

'No. No, Carole's gone off on an expedition to Pinara.'

'Really? Well, there's a coincidence.'

'Oh?'

'Phyllis and I were thinking of going over in that direction today.'

'Ah.'

'There's a little restaurant we quite like up in a village near there. I'd thought we might go there for lunch . . . but Phyllis says she doesn't feel up to it.'

'I'm sorry.'

'There's not much she does feel up to these days. It was probably rather foolish of me to imagine that she might be able to accompany me.'

'Well, there you go . . .' said Jude fatuously.

'Yes. So I was just wondering . . .'

'Mm?'

'. . . whether you'd like to come with me?'

'For lunch?'

'Yes. Give you an opportunity to see a bit of the surrounding area. It's very beautiful.'

'Well, Travers, that's terribly kind of you, but I had really planned just a lazy day by the pool.'

'Oh, very well,' he said. 'Another time, perhaps?'

Over my dead body, thought Jude.

Pinara was not what Carole Seddon would have regarded as an archaeological site. The ones she'd been to in England had all been protected like Fort Knox, with guard rails and grilles everywhere. Nobody was allowed to wander off the authorized routes. Health and Safety was clearly higher up the organizers' priorities than historical interest.

Whereas Pinara seemed to be open to everyone. True, there was a small wooden hut near the car park, beside which a small motor scooter was drawn up. From the amiable man inside she bought a rather attractively decorated ticket about the size of a five-pound note. But it didn't look as if it would be difficult to get into the site illegally if one wished to (something which, of course, Carole Seddon never would wish). But apart from the odd signpost there was little in the way of official intervention into how one wished to conduct one's visit. And, so far as she could see, there were no areas roped off.

As she'd stepped out of the Fiat in the car park, Carole had had two dominant feelings. One was, as she felt the almost brutal impact of the heat, that she was very glad she'd bought the straw hat.

And second was a sensation of satisfaction that was almost gleeful. She had managed it. She had found her way to Pinara. The start of the journey, it was true, had not been easy. The narrow roads, the unfamiliar car, driving on the right in a foreign country, all of those factors had contributed to state that was close to panic. Until she got through the tangled traffic of Fethiye, in spite of the air conditioning, she had been sweating like a pig and felt that her bladder was about to burst.

But gradually, the further she progressed on the expedition, the calmer she became. And she gained confidence from the efficiency of her navigational skills. They had always been one of her secret sources of pride. Carole Seddon would never set out on a journey without having made a thorough study of the route beforehand. She had an instinctive memory for road numbers and target destinations. She could visualize a route rolling out before her, knowing which place name she had to aim for, which villages she would have to drive through to get there.

During their marriage her husband David, a nit-picker and minor control freak in many ways, had never challenged her superiority as a navigator. On the few uneasy holidays they'd taken in France with the silent teenage Stephen, David had driven with Carole at his side, map on her lap, as reliable as a homing pigeon. In such situations, though not many others, her ex-husband had known his place.

So, to have negotiated the wild terrain and unfamiliar sign-posting between Kayaköy and Pinara gave a huge boost to Carole's confidence. As she neared the destination, she felt positively buoyant. She was no longer sweating, the air conditioning had done its work, and when she drew the Fiat up beside a purple tourist coach in the car park she had completely forgotten how desperately, a mere half an hour before, she had wanted to find a loo.

There was only the one coach. It was empty. The lift-up door to the baggage compartment had been raised on one side, and in the shade the driver slept peacefully on a blanket. Apart from the Fiat there were only a couple of other cars parked. It wasn't the height of the tourist season, but Carole wondered if even then this remote hilltop ever got crowded.

From where she was looking, though the foothills of the cylindrical mountain were wooded, there wasn't a lot of shade on the rest of the site. So, characteristically cautious, she rubbed more of the Factor Fifty on to her exposed arms, face and particularly the back of her neck. She picked up the bottle of water she'd bought at the supermarket and put it in the Morning Glory cool bag she'd thoughtfully brought with her. With that in her knapsack and the money belt rather uncomfortably about her waist she felt ready for her expedition.

She left the *Rough Guide* in the car. She had been through the relevant couple of pages so many times that she virtually knew them off by heart.

Then, with her ticket bought and holding the small fold-up map she'd been given at the shed, she set off to sample the mysteries of Pinara.

The whole vast area was dominated by a huge mountain, almost cylindrical and cut across like the trunk of some giant felled tree. Its cliffs, though Carole was not yet close enough to see, she knew would be pockmarked by rectangular Lycian tombs cut into the rock.

From the entrance, a track led up the lazy incline round the edge of the circular outcrop. Carole knew, if she followed it, that she could access the Lower Acropolis to the left and the Amphitheatre to the right. Whether later on she'd have the energy to face the long climb to the Upper Acropolis she would have to wait and see.

The only nearby wooded area was to the left of the entrance, but the air was still warmly scented with pine and thyme. It was early enough in the year for a few wild flowers to be in evidence and the unexpected change of scene built up the confidence engendered by her successful journey there. It seemed bizarre to remember that she'd left Fethering only the morning before.

That thought prompted a vision of Gulliver and a slight pang for him. How he would love to be with her in this exotic environment, roaming free to investigate so many unfamiliar smells. Then again, she thought, how miserable he would be in this intense heat.

Carole had decided that she would have a look at the Amphitheatre before the Lower Acropolis, but when she got near enough, she saw a swarm of tourists there. Presumably, the ones from the purple bus. As ever wary of human company, she started the climb to the Lower Acropolis.

The way up was steep, but Carole Seddon carried no excess weight on her thin frame so the effort didn't feel too bad. But she did find herself wondering how the more substantial Jude might have coped. It was a good idea all round that they'd decided to spend the day apart.

The path levelled out, and Carole stopped to take another swig of water. The cool bag was doing its stuff, and it still felt chilled enough to be refreshing. She looked at her watch. It was nearly one o'clock, and she felt her stomach rumble. Breakfast seemed a long time ago, and the provisions she had bought were in the car. But Carole was not about to cut short her exploration of Pinara for something as trivial as hunger.

She climbed a little further and came to a flat area littered with square-cut stones. Some of them stood regularly upon others, showing the traces of walls and outlines of buildings. Others were scattered round like a toddler's Lego. There were a couple of crumbled standing tombs, like the one they'd gone round in the middle of the road leading out of Fethiye. Discoloured rusting notices, white painted letters on dark-blue in Turkish and English, identified one particular area as a temple but, overgrown by trees and shrubbery as it was, Carole couldn't make out the shape of it.

Until her crash course of the last few weeks' reading she had never heard of the Lycian civilization, and even now she wouldn't have claimed to be an expert. Nor could she ever

have claimed to have much interest in archaeology. But she
was very glad she had decided to come to Pinara that day.

There was something about the place. Carole was glad Jude
wasn't there because her head was filling with words that
she usually pooh-poohed. Words like 'magic', 'enchantment',
'atmosphere', even 'aura'.

It was just the sheer antiquity of the place that was getting
to her. The sight of these huge blocks of stone, hewn out of
the living rock by men who lacked any kind of power tools,
was somehow inspiring. And, at the same time, daunting. The
toppling structures around her made Carole think of both the
durability of human ambition and the inevitability of human
failure. It made her considerably more introspective than was
her custom. And, to her considerable annoyance, it made her
feel as though she was in the presence of a power stronger
than her own.

To banish such nonsense from her mind she took another
long swig from her water bottle and set off back down to the
main track. Though the gradient was easier, the stones had
been rendered glassy by generations of footsteps and it was a
slightly precarious descent.

Carole felt even hungrier, and the sun through her hat felt
even hotter, but there was no way she was going to return to
the car without seeing the Amphitheatre. So she left the track
and walked towards it across a flat field full of some Turkish
form of thistle (she was glad she hadn't gone for the shorts
option, otherwise her legs would have been shredded).

As she approached the structure, she encountered the busload of tourists weaving their sweaty way back towards the
car park. Once within earshot she quickly recognized that they
were English and bridled accordingly. Though there were no
Union Jack T-shirts or tattoos in evidence – in fact, this
appeared to be a rather genteel, mature and well-heeled selection of her countrymen – Carole felt no urgency to engage in
conversation with them. All they got was a tight smile and a
'Fethering nod' – a small inclination of the head, the most
minimal anonymous form of acknowledgement possible.

The group was led by a Turkish man wearing white trousers
and a pale-blue polo shirt bearing the logo of some travel

company. 'But where's she gone to?' Carole heard a woman asking him as she walked by. The accent was unappealingly Midlands. This must be the group from Kidderminster that Nita had referred to.

'I am sure she has not gone far,' the guide replied in good English. 'We will meet her at the bus. If not there, she will be back at the hotel.'

'Well, it's rather important because I wanted to ask her about the toilet in our bathroom which has got blocked, which is . . .' And the woman's voice drifted past into inaudibility.

The Amphitheatre was impressive and in a surprisingly good state of preservation. From her memorized guidebook notes, Carole knew that it was probably of Roman construction though built in the Greek horseshoe style, and it could seat over three thousand. She marvelled at its design and durability as she climbed up to the back row. It was a place that encouraged conjectures about the people who might have come there, the entertainments they might have seen, but it didn't prompt in Carole any of the mystical sensation that she had felt by the temple. Thank goodness.

From her vantage point she looked across at the huge cylinder of rock opposite. Its sheer size made her glad she had not tried to climb any further than the Lower Acropolis. She could see the honeycomb of tombs carved into the sheer cliff and comforted herself that they were not accessible to tourists. For a moment she wondered whether she should have brought a camera, but she quickly comforted herself with the recollection that she always took rubbish photographs and never looked at the ones she had taken on her return from a holiday. The only photographs that interested her now were of her granddaughter. And thinking of Lily made her wonder how things were back in Fulham. She hadn't set up her laptop yet at Morning Glory, but she must email Stephen that evening.

Carole was now distinctly peckish and feeling a little dazed by the bright sunlight. She felt she had done enough sightseeing to justify a return to the car park and her modest rations of bread, salami and tomatoes. Whether she would explore more of Pinara after lunch she rather doubted.

But, trudging along the track, she had a slightly guilty feeling that there was one more feature of the site she should visit. Though the cliff-side tombs could only be explored from a distance with binoculars, the *Rough Guide* had told her that there were some on the west side of a small stream quite near the site entrance. These included what was called the 'Royal Tomb', whose elaborate carvings were well worth seeing.

Being so close, Carole decided to put her hunger pangs on hold a little longer and investigate.

Arrows on metal signs pointed the way. The area around the tiny stream was overgrown with trees which provided a pleasant dappled relief from the sun, now so hot that it almost stung Carole's arms. Some of the trees had fallen to provide a precarious bridge over the water, but in fact it was so shallow that she could have waded through.

As she stepped forward on to a horizontal branch, she was aware of a slight movement in the undergrowth beneath her feet. She looked down to see a tortoise making its laborious but determined way through the scrub. A tortoise in its natural environment, nobody's pet (indeed, they were no longer allowed to be kept as pets in England, she recalled). It made her feel that she was really abroad.

Carole climbed up the rocks on the other side of the stream and suddenly emerged into sunlight. And there, just one level up on the rock face, was a row of carved-out Lycian tombs. She clambered up the uneven path until she was standing in front of one.

It looked remarkably solid, like a small house carved out of the pale, vanilla-coloured stone. There were pillars at each end, one somewhat battered, and a series of carved frames on the building's double frontage. One side was walled in, though a hole had at some point (maybe by grave robbers or vandals) been smashed into it. The other side was open like a doorway.

Carole had to stoop to get under the stone lintel. There was enough light for her to see that she was in an austere rectangular cell. Along the far wall ran a rectangular stone slab almost like a bench or a bed. The image was exactly like the pictures of Lycian tombs in the guidebooks Carole had been so assiduously reading.

Except that there was someone lying on the slab. A woman, the red and blue lanyard of whose identity card had been twisted around her neck until she died.

It was Nita.

FOURTEEN

B y the time Carole got back to the Fiat Bravo she had forgotten all about being hungry. She had been unsure whether she should immediately report her discovery to the man who had sold her the ticket, but that decision was made for her. The shed from which he'd operated was closed up, and the motor scooter beside it had disappeared.

The purple bus had gone from the car park too. Apart from the Fiat only two cars remained. Their owners were presumably somewhere on the site, but Carole could see no sign of them. Maybe they were among the brave and fit ones who had climbed all the way to the Upper Acropolis.

Carole was in a dilemma. Her training in the Home Office and every other instinct within her said that any murder should be reported to the police as soon as possible. And had the ticket man been there in his shed she would have gone straight to him and set the necessary process in motion. But he wasn't there and that had given her time to think.

So what should she do? Contacting the police should not be too difficult. She had her mobile with her and though she didn't think 999 was going to work, she felt sure there was some equivalent number to ring which she could find out when she got to some less remote part of the country.

But did she actually want to get involved in the laborious business of waiting around for the police, of leading them back to Nita's body, and then no doubt undergoing long questioning, probably made even longer by the necessity of an interpreter? It all seemed too much.

And then she didn't really feel sure about the authorities that she'd be up against. Although she had never actually seen the film *Midnight Express*, Carole had gathered that it wasn't the most enthusiastic commercial ever for the Turkish police force. (And she didn't know of the subsequent international row about the portrayal of Turks in the movie which even led to an apology from the screenwriter.) But such ignorant prejudices go deep with people like Carole Seddon, and the dominant question that arose in her mind was: did she really want to get involved?

She would have felt very differently if Jude had been with her when she discovered the body. Then they could have discussed the situation and worked out their next step together. But, on her own in the car park at Pinara, she felt desperately isolated.

Yes, she definitely needed Jude's input.

Had she thought about it, Carole would have been impressed with the way she drove back to Kayaköy, like someone who'd been on Turkish roads all her life. The fact was, she was so preoccupied by what she'd found in the tomb at Pinara that she couldn't think about anything else. Her driving was purely instinctive.

She found Jude more or less exactly as she had left her, spread over a lounger in a bikini with a trashy novel at her side. The book had already taken on those qualities of heat-crinkled paper and suncream stains which distinguish a holiday read.

It took a minute or two for the seriousness of Carole's news to permeate Jude's torpor. But once she'd taken it on board, she had no hesitation in agreeing to her friend's proposal that they should return immediately to the scene of the crime. And, as Carole had anticipated, Jude didn't go for any of that nonsense about informing the police first.

The morning expedition from Kayaköy to Pinara had taken nearly an hour and a half, as Carole had driven with extreme caution, rarely aspiring beyond second gear, but on the second journey she couldn't help being rather proud of her proficiency, almost showing it off. As a result, they reached their destination in little more than an hour.

It was after five when they arrived, and the car park was empty. The intrepid souls who had possibly climbed to the Higher Acropolis had returned to their hotels or villas to shower off the day's dust.

No one arriving at Pinara for the first time could fail to be struck by the beauty of the site, but Jude made no comment on the vista before her. Their mission was too serious for such pleasantries.

Carole had no hesitation about the path they had to take. The sun was still bright, but it had lost some of its midday intensity. The shade of the trees by the little stream was nonetheless welcome.

Carole led the way along the tree-trunk bridge. This time there was no tortoise to distract her. She pointed out to Jude the tombs above them and scrambled over the time-polished stones to reach them.

She gestured to the doorway of the relevant tomb, indicating that Jude should enter first.

Which she did. But she was taken aback by what she saw in there.

The stone slab was empty. Nita's body had disappeared.

FIFTEEN

They looked for any signs to prove that the body had been there, but found nothing. No tell-tale snagged thread of fabric, no stain of bodily fluid. Perhaps a properly equipped police forensic team could have found something, but to their amateur eyes no traces revealed themselves.

The one thing that never occurred to Jude was to question Carole's report of what she had seen. There were women of her acquaintance prone to hysteria, women quite capable of convincing themselves they'd seen things that were never there, but Carole Seddon was not one of them. If Carole said she had seen Nita Davies's body in the Lycian tomb where they stood, then that was exactly what had happened.

So they were certain of two things. One, that the body had been there. And two, that in the course of the last four hours someone had removed it.

There was little more they could do at the empty scene of the crime. Carole was confused between guilt and relief. If she had tried to report her discovery to the police they might have got there in time to capture the body snatcher (who, quite possibly, was also the murderer). But now, since there was no body to report, she had probably saved herself a whole lot of aggravation.

With that thought, however, came another one. There was no doubt that a murder had been committed. And Carole knew that she shared with Jude an overpowering instinct to find out who had perpetrated the crime.

They checked the adjacent tombs – or, at least, the ones they could get into – but the only signs there of human habitation were the odd Efes can and crisp packet. As they began to trail disconsolately into the woods on their way back towards the car park, though, Jude caught sight of something bright trapped against some trailing twigs in the stream.

Clumsily, she lowered herself down to pick up the object. It was a mobile: an iPhone in a light-blue case with a dark-blue fish design.

'Nita's!' exclaimed Carole as it was held up for her inspection. 'I recognize that from when she used it at Morning Glory. It must have slipped out of her pocket when her body was being moved.' The discovery gave her a warm glow. It was a kind of proof that, though she had subsequently been relocated, Nita had definitely passed that way. The mobile linked her to the scene of the crime.

Jude was already tapping at the screen to check for messages. But all she found was a ten-number keyboard and an invitation to 'Enter Passcode'.

'Damn,' she said.

As Carole negotiated the traffic of Fethiye like someone who'd been doing it all her life, the sun was sinking in the sky. 'Be dark in half an hour,' said Jude. 'What I'd really like to do is have a look at the Kayaköy ghost town while it's still light.'

'Should we be doing that?' asked Carole.

'What do you mean?'

'Well, having just seen a body . . .'

'Having just not seen a body, in my case.'

'What I mean is: shouldn't we be doing something other than just sightseeing?'

'Like what? Contacting the police?'

But no, that was not what Carole had in mind. She had once before summoned the police to a place where she had discovered a body, only to find that all traces had disappeared, and she hadn't forgotten the patronizing scepticism with which they had treated her. That incident had occurred on Fethering Beach, but she didn't think she'd encounter any less disbelief from the police in Turkey. So she turned down Jude's suggestion.

'Well what else do you want to do? Talk to Barney? See if we can track down Erkan?'

'Good heavens, no. You and I just need to talk through what's happened.'

'Seems to me a ghost town is just as good a place to talk as anywhere else.'

In the dusty flat area at the foot of the ghost town were a cluster of fairly primitive looking restaurants, one graffitied over with fluorescent symbols which gave it a sixties hippy feel. And, incongruously, there was a man with three camels. Presumably, during the high tourist season he peddled rides on the beasts to tourists, but that Tuesday evening he wasn't getting much trade. The camels, tethered to trees, chomped away, showing no interest in anything.

Carole parked the Bravo in a space outside one of the restaurants, but nobody came out to dragoon them into its vine-ceilinged open space to have a meal. Having been warned by her guidebooks that it was impossible to pause for a moment on a street in Istanbul without being immediately approached by men trying to sell you carpets or get you into their restaurants, she found Kayaköy mercifully free of aggressive marketing.

They walked round the edge of the furthest restaurant and found the entrance to the ghost town site. There was a small ticket booth there, but it was empty. Presumably, few people visited in the twilight. But, as at Pinara, there were no gates, nothing to stop them entering if they wished to.

A small sign in English pointed right towards a small church, but the two friends went left up the worn stone steps into the ghost town itself. Above them, the buildings climbed the hillside in neat tiers. The houses were stone-built and solid. Their roofs had all fallen in long ago, but only a few dwellings had collapsed completely, and there was no sign of vandalism. The evening air was perfumed by pine and thyme. Wild flowers grew up in the crevices between the stones.

Carole once again reaped the benefit of her guidebook homework. 'It all goes back to 1923. The people who lived here up till then were Anatolian Greek Orthodox Christians . . .'

'Right,' said Jude, feeling as if she was back at school and undergoing a history lesson. 'Didn't Henry Willingdon tell us most of this stuff when we were at Chantry House?'

'Not all the detail,' said Carole in her most severe schoolmistress mode. 'It was part of the settlement that came about after the end of the Greco-Turkish War.'

'I didn't know there was a Greco-Turkish War.'

'You see? Henry didn't tell us about that, did she? The Greco-Turkish War lasted from 1919 to 1922. Rather nasty war, many atrocities. But though the Greeks took over lots of bits of the old Ottoman Empire during the war, when they admitted defeat all the territory went back to the Turks. And very soon after that the Ottoman Empire was abolished and the Turkish Republic was created, under Kemal Atatürk. Then the "Convention concerning the Exchange of Greek and Turkish Populations" was signed in Lausanne in Switzerland, which made—'

'Which made,' Jude interrupted, 'the Greek and the Turkish populations of the territories go back, respectively, to Greece and Turkey?'

'Well,' said Carole, a little miffed at having her lecture curtailed, 'that's rather a simplification of what happened, but it's more or less right.'

'Except that none of the Muslims who'd been living in Greek territories ever came back here to Kayaköy?'

'No, they didn't.'

'Which is why this place is a ghost town?'

'Yes,' Carole conceded grudgingly, regretting that her neighbour had been treated to only a small amount of the detail that she had at her fingertips.

They walked for a while in silence on the stone paths between the houses, looking in at fireplaces, interior doorways and collapsed rafters. The evacuation of the town seemed somehow much more recent than 1923. Carole was, for a moment, almost in danger of once again experiencing the feeling that she had undergone at Pinara, an empathy with the people who had once inhabited these stone houses, the sense that the ghost town had an 'aura'.

She quickly suppressed such foolishness and said, as if it had been Jude who'd initiated the history lecture, 'Anyway, I thought we were having this walk to discuss Nita's murder.'

Jude grinned, not for the first time, at the Caroleness of Carole. 'Yes. I'm with you about not going to the police. Do you think we should talk to Barney?'

Carole shook her head. 'I don't think so.'

'Because you believe he might be a suspect?'

'No, not really. Though he has got dubious secrets in his past.'

'Like exactly what happened to his first wife, Zoë?'

'Yes.' Carole grimaced. 'No, my view is, frustrating though it may be, that at this moment we should just do nothing.'

'Not tell anyone what you saw?'

Another shake of the head. 'Not yet, no. If we meet Barney or Erkan or Henry we can certainly keep an eye on their behaviour, but—'

'Henry? I thought Henry was safely back in Chantry House in Sussex.'

'No.' And Carole proceeded to tell Jude about her sighting of Barney's wife in Fethiye. But her description of Henry's male companion was too vague for Jude to identify him as Fergus McNally. 'I think all we can do,' Carole concluded, 'is to keep a watching brief on any of them we do meet. It won't be for long.'

'How do you mean?' asked Jude.

'Nita's been murdered. Soon, her body's going to be found. And even if it's been successfully hidden away somewhere, people are pretty soon going to realize that she's missing. Her husband, Erkan, apart from anyone else.'

It was nearly dark when the two women got back down to the car and the camels. Carole showed only token resistance when Jude suggested they have a drink – and, come to that, eat dinner – in one of the restaurants. They chose one called Antik.

Inside, they could have sprawled on one of the circular rug- and cushion-covered platforms, the modern equivalent of the old Turkish *divan*, but Carole resolutely steered them towards a four-seater table. There were quite a few people around, but more seemed to be the management's family members than diners. In spite of the outside temperature, a wood fire burned, and in front of it knelt a couple of women in traditional patterned trousers and headscarves. They poured batter on to circular hotplates, then shaped the fluid with wooden spatulas until it crisped into pancakes.

'*Gözleme*,' said Carole authoritatively.

'Bless you,' said Jude, misunderstanding.

'No, they're making *gözleme*. "Village pancakes." Don't you remember? Nita told us about them when we were driving over.'

'Oh, yes, they look rather good.'

A smiling, casually dressed man in his forties wandered over to their table. Carole tried desperately to summon up some of the phrase-book sentences she had learned for 'In The Restaurant'. Before she had time to speak, though, the man had said, 'Good evening,' in accented but perfect English and asked what they would like to drink.

To Carole's surprise, Jude asked for a large Efes beer.

'Draught?'

'Yes, please. We've just walked up to the ghost town. Hot work.' And, indeed, Jude's round red face gleamed with sweat.

'You chose a good time to do it. In the middle of the day, too hot. So, one large beer. And for you, madam?'

'A glass of white wine, please. Do you have a Chardonnay?' asked Carole instinctively.

'No, madam. We have local white wine. Very good. It's from a Turkish grape you would not know, but it tastes very like Sauvignon Blanc.'

'Oh, I'll try that, thank you.'

'Just a glass or a small carafe?'

'Just a glass, thank you.'

'Oh, let's go for a large carafe,' said Jude. 'I'll be moving on to the wine once I've finished my beer.'

'But I don't think—'

Carole's words seemed to be unheard. 'Very good, a large carafe of local white wine. And will you be eating as well?'

'Oh, yes, you bet,' said Jude.

'I will bring you menus. But let me say I have some very good lamb cutlets in today, if you like them, and some fresh sea bass.'

'And *gözleme*.' Carole, pleased to show off her Turkish, gestured towards the women at the fire.

'And, of course, *gözleme*. These can be filled with cheese and spinach or ground beef or roasted eggplant.' His use of the last word, instead of 'aubergine', demonstrated that some of his tourist customers were American as well as English.

He barked out a command in Turkish, and a fourteen-year-old boy with short-cropped black hair who'd been squatting by the fireplace immediately brought across two menus. The likeness was so striking that he had to be the owner's son. The menus, they found, were in Turkish, English and German, indicating the range of expected visitors.

'I will get your drinks,' said his owner, 'and then take your order for food.' An instruction went out to another short-haired, but slightly older son, who immediately came across with a basket of cutlery and condiments and fitted a paper tablecloth over the table's wooden surface. He secured it under elastic strings which ran beneath the tabletop.

By the time he had finished, his father had returned with the drinks. Both beer glass and wine carafe sparkled with condensation from the fridge.

'Ooh, that looks so wonderful,' said Jude, taking a long slurp of the pale yellow beer. 'Aah, bliss . . .'

Carole found the first sip of wine that the man had poured for her equally welcome. Again, it was a change from the buttery Chardonnay she so often drank in the Crown and Anchor. But not an unwelcome change.

The man took their orders. Carole liked the sound of the *gözleme* with cheese and spinach, while Jude opted for the lamb cutlets.

'*Pirzola*,' said the owner. 'Very good.'

'We ought to have some starters too,' said Jude. 'What do you fancy, Carole?'

'Oh, I don't really know whether I actually need—'

'Let's have the *cacik* and some *dolma*.'

'Very good,' said the man. 'And please, you are the ladies from Morning Glory – yes?'

As they admitted they were, Carole and Jude exchanged looks. There certainly were no secrets in Kayaköy.

After the owner was out of earshot, Carole whispered, 'I didn't know you spoke Turkish.'

'Sorry?'

'You just ordered those starters without looking at the menu.'

'That hardly qualifies as "speaking Turkish".'

'So does this mean you've been to Turkey before?'

'Yes.'

'Why didn't you tell me?'

'You didn't ask.'

SIXTEEN

The beer and wine did their work, and by the time their main courses arrived Carole felt almost relaxed. She reflected that it had been quite a stressful day – a stressful few days, in fact. All the business of leaving to go on holiday, arriving in Turkey, adjusting to Morning Glory and sleeping so badly there. Then dealing with an unfamiliar car on alien roads. Add to all that the shock of finding – and then losing – Nita's body, and it was no wonder she had felt tense.

But she knew her improved mood was not just due to the alcohol. Gruesome though it might seem to some people, Carole was also experiencing that little *frisson* of excitement that always came at the beginning of a murder investigation. She looked across at Jude draining the last of the beer and knew that her friend was feeling the same.

Her *gözleme* had arrived rolled into cigar shapes on a bed of salad. The way she'd fallen on the pitta bread with the starters made Carole realize how hungry she was (she'd never got round to eating her salami lunch). And she'd discovered that *cacik* was the Turkish version of the Greek *tzatziki* and *dolma* were stuffed vine leaves. Both delicious. Carole Seddon was beginning to think she might have underestimated the qualities of Turkish cuisine.

There was a silence as they addressed their main courses, which was broken by the approach of Barney Willingdon. They had been aware in their peripheral vision of a white Range Rover drawing up outside Antik but hadn't really registered it as his until Barney spoke.

'Evening, ladies. I found Morning Glory all closed up, so I assumed you'd be down in one of the restaurants. And since most people have the ghost town as number one on their itinerary in Kayaköy, I reckoned here was a good place to start.'

'And you won a coconut first time,' said Jude.

'Exactly.' He waved a friendly hand to the restaurant owner. 'Hi, Ahmet. A large Efes, please.' But there was something different in his manner. He was presenting his 'hail fellow, well met' Barney Willingdon persona, but it didn't sound as convincing as usual. He was sweating more than the warm evening justified, he kept scratching nervously at his beard, and his eyes seemed to be darting around on the lookout for someone or something. Was he worried about another attack from Kemal, or another of the enemies his business practices had made? Or did his unease have something to do with the death of Nita Davies?

'Are you eating too?' asked Carole, not sure that she wanted their tête-à-tête interrupted, but at the same time aware that to make any progress in their investigation they must, at some point, talk to Barney.

'No, had a late lunch. I'll maybe grab something back at the villa. Anyway, how did you ladies spend your first full day in Kayaköy?'

'We went our separate ways,' said Jude. 'Or, rather, I didn't go any way at all. I just stayed and lounged by the pool until we came out here at dusk to have a look at the ghost town.'

Jude's brown eyes were flashing messages to Carole while she said this, and they were immediately understood. No mention of the second trip to Pinara. No mention indeed of the discovery made on the first trip to Pinara. With regard to Nita, they would wait until Barney volunteered something.

'And what about you, Carole?'

'I did a bit of sightseeing.'

'Good. In the car?'

'Yes.'

'Didn't give you any problems, I hope?'

'Worked beautifully, thank you.'

'Good. So where did you go?'

Carole eyed him shrewdly, watchful for any reaction when she said the word, 'Pinara.'

There was none. 'Lovely spot,' he said. 'I've spent some very happy times there.'

'Yes.' And then Carole dared to add, 'Nita recommended it to me.'

'As I said, she knows the area like the back of her hand.'

'Yes, she gave us lots of good ideas yesterday of places to go,' said Jude.

'She would.'

'But we haven't seen her today,' Jude continued casually.

'No.' Barney looked very uncomfortable. 'And you won't see her for a while.'

Carole and Jude both managed very effectively to hide their shock at his words.

'Oh, why's that?' asked Carole.

'She's had to fly back to England,' said Barney. 'Her mother's ill.'

'We were right not to ask him any more,' said Carole.

They were sitting on the upstairs balcony of Morning Glory,

which was accessible from both their bedrooms. Carole's doors were wide open; Jude had closed hers so that the air conditioning could take some effect before she went to bed. Carole had a glass of water; Jude more white wine from the fridge.

'Hm?' Jude said.

'If Barney did know about Nita's death and was just lying to us, then we didn't want him to know we were suspicious of him. If he didn't know, then equally we didn't want to raise his suspicions.'

'And are we suspicious of him?'

'I think we have to be. Clearly, there's been something going on between him and Nita.'

'What makes you say that?'

'Oh, come on, Jude. Last night at that barbecue place she was clearly offering herself to him, and he was equally clearly declining the offer. You don't have conversations like that unless there's something going on.'

Jude nodded. Sometimes Carole could be very perceptive. And Jude recognized that there was something within her that didn't want to admit the relationship between Barney and Nita might still be carrying on. Though the feeling couldn't be defined as strongly as jealousy, it still niggled at her.

A silence lingered between them. Both sipped their drinks. Then Carole said pensively, 'It's so strange. What happened this morning was almost like a dream . . . you know, finding Nita's body out in the wilds of Pinara . . . which, incidentally, certainly *did* happen.' Her tone became defensive on the last few words.

'I've never doubted it happened,' said Jude soothingly. 'You're the least likely person I know to be subject to hysterical delusions.'

Carole wasn't quite sure whether that was a compliment or not, but she hadn't got time to question it. 'But as a coincidence it's a pretty huge one, isn't it? I mean, that I should be in Pinara . . .'

'Who knew you were going to go there?'

'Well, nobody knew for certain because, in fact, I only made up my mind this morning. But I did mention the possibility of going at that barbecue place last night.'

'So Nita knew.'

'Yes, but I don't think she set up her own murder specifically so that I could discover her body,' said Carole with an edge of sarcasm.

'No, but I was thinking she might have told someone else that you might be going to Pinara.'

'Like who?'

'Her husband? And then, of course, that was just before Kemal came on to the scene. He might have overheard you talking about Pinara.'

Carole sniffed. 'Possible, I suppose, but unlikely.' There was a silence before she continued, 'And then, of course, there's Barney.'

'Yes.' Jude sighed. 'And then, of course, there's Barney . . .'

They went to bed soon after that. Carole waited until she thought Jude might be asleep and not hear before she closed all her bedroom windows and switched on the air conditioning. She didn't want to sleep as badly as she had the previous night.

SEVENTEEN

The air conditioning did the trick, and Carole slept much better. When she woke at seven she almost felt too cold, but she was fully prepared to forget for the next fortnight her mother's diktat that she 'should never go to sleep without at least one window open'. Now she was awake, though, she switched off the air conditioning and opened up everything. Heat soon replaced the chill, and the long net curtains swayed in a light breeze. Curling round the window frames, she saw the delicate blue of the Morning Glory.

Carole moved out on to the balcony. The sky was unbroken blue with the promise of another perfect day. As she looked down over the pool she thought she saw a sudden movement in the trees that edged the track down to the village, but it wasn't repeated. Just a bird, probably. Or a local cat. Or the latter chasing the former.

There was no sound from Jude's room, and Carole had the daring thought that she might put on her costume and try the delights of the pool. Why not? She was on holiday. So she took off her nightdress and slipped on the Marks & Spencer dark-blue number, careful all the while not to see any reflections of her body in the bedroom's generous mirrors. Then she anointed every uncovered bit of skin with the Factor Fifty before, stepping into her flip-flops and picking up a bright bathing towel, she made her way downstairs.

Carole Seddon couldn't begin to remember how long it was since she had last swum. There were hardy residents who regularly braved the cement-coloured waters of Fethering Beach, but she had never been of their number. She had paddled around in the shallows when she'd spent a week with her granddaughter Lily at nearby Smalting, but when had she last undergone total immersion? No, the memory had gone (though the memory remained of shivering round the municipal pool for school swimming lessons with the overpowering smell of chlorine in her nose).

By comparison, she was surprised how pleasant the experience was in Kayaköy. Unheated but exposed daily to the Turkish sun, the water was as warm as a bath, and the setting was heavenly. Blue sky overhead, the villa swamped by the paler blue of the Morning Glory and the infinite horizon at the edge of the pool. But for the troubling consciousness of Nita Davies's murder, everything was perfect. And to someone of Carole Seddon's mindset even the murder was a kind of positive – a puzzle to be solved.

Whereas Jude had spent most of the previous day just lolling in the pool, taking the occasional desultory few strokes, Carole had immediately started swimming lengths – and counting them. She even counted the number of strokes each length took and started multiplying the totals. When she had done five hundred in her earnest, childlike breaststroke she got out of the pool and reached for her towel. At that point Jude – and most other human beings, to be quite honest – would have laid down on a lounger for the sun to complete the natural drying process. But Carole's first instinct was to dry herself off with the towel – so that she didn't drip over the inside of Morning Glory – and go straight indoors to change out of her costume.

She was, however, prevented from achieving this by the appearance of Travers Hughes-Swann, whom she had observed from her bedroom window accosting Jude on their first afternoon at the villa. He was wearing exactly the same clothes as he had been on that occasion. The leathery skin of his chest and arms made him look like some prehistoric man excavated from a Danish bog.

'You must be the missing Carole,' he said.

She was slightly unnerved by the promptness of his appearance. It was almost as if he'd been waiting till she got out of the pool to come and introduce himself. Surely, the movement in the trees she'd seen from her balcony hadn't been Travers lurking, keeping Morning Glory under surveillance? It was an uncomfortable thought.

She admitted that she was indeed Carole.

'I met your friend Jude.'

'Yes, she mentioned that.'

'And I gather you went off yesterday to enjoy the delights of Pinara.'

How the hell did he know that? But Carole didn't voice the thought. Not knowing that Jude had told him, she thought it was just more evidence that there were no secrets in Kayaköy.

'How did you like the place?'

'Very striking.'

'And what struck you in particular?'

'Well, I suppose, the tombs.'

'Which ones?'

'The ones carved out of the sheer mountain face, the ones you can't get to. Not the kind of sight we're used to in England.'

'No. Whereabouts is it in England you hail from? Jude didn't say.'

'Little village called Fethering. On the South Coast.'

'Fethering, yes. Never been there, but I've seen signs for it.'

'Oh?'

'Phyllis and I used to live in Southampton. Phyllis, I should have said, is "Her Indoors" – very much so, I'm afraid, these days. Bedridden.'

Carole murmured some mumble of condolence.

'So she's "Her Indoors" and I'm "Him Outdoors". Spend all my time gardening.'

Carole didn't recognize this, but it was a half-joke everyone who met Travers had to undergo.

'Yes, we used to see signs to Fethering when we drove along the A27 towards Brighton.'

'Ah.' Carole was beginning to feel extremely uncomfortable. The man was apparently quite happy to stand by the pool maundering away all morning. And he was openly looking at legs that had been very rarely seen in the last decade. Not to mention her cleavage, of which her bathing costume offered a more generous allocation than allowed by the rest of her wardrobe.

Purposely, she picked up her bathing towel. 'I must go in and get dressed.'

'Yes, of course. I won't stop you. Just to say, if there's anything I can do to help, I'm only next door.'

'Thank you. That's very kind.'

'And maybe we could meet up for a drink and a chat at some point . . .?'

Carole's reaction to the proposal exactly mirrored Jude's of the previous morning. *Over my dead body.*

'I think we should go to Hisarönü,' announced Jude. They were breakfasting together on an area of the patio shaded by a network of vines and Morning Glory. Jude had appeared in yet another bikini just after Travers left. They'd finished up the fruit from the fridge and toasted the remains of the bread. Whatever else they did during the day, a visit to the super-market to stock up on essentials would have to be fitted in.

'Why Hisarönü?' asked Carole, prejudiced by what her guidebooks and Nita had said about the place. Unwelcome images of Union Jack T-shirts and tattoos invaded her mind.

'Because we need to find out anything we can about Nita Davies, and we happen to know that her friend works there.'

'Ah, the Dirty Duck.'

'Exactly. Nita's friend Donna who we met briefly at Dalaman Airport.'

'I think the flyer she gave us is still in my bag upstairs.'

'If it isn't, we still should be able to find the place. There aren't going to be two restaurants called the Dirty Duck in a Turkish village.'

'From what I've read about Hisarönü,' said Carole beadily, 'I wouldn't rule out the possibility. And, of course, the other person who should be able to tell us lots about Nita is her husband.'

'Erkan?'

'Right. She said there was something about his diving school in the villa's welcome pack.'

'And that's in Ölüdeniz, isn't it?'

'Yes,' said Carole, confident of the local maps that she had memorized. 'So we'd better take the details with us because Ölüdeniz is only a few miles beyond Hisarönü.' She piled up their two toast plates. 'Right, we'd better be off then.'

'No, let's spend the morning by the pool. The Dirty Duck won't be open yet.'

'Donna said it did full English breakfasts. I'm sure it'll be open.'

'Oh, it'll be nicer to have the morning by the pool. Then we can go and have lunch at the Dirty Duck.'

Carole would have liked to be up and doing straight away, but she graciously didn't argue. Instead, she spent the morning in cotton top and trousers sitting rather stiffly on a lounger and working on one of her *Times* crosswords, while Jude alternated between sploshing in the pool and reading her trashy novel.

Eventually (for Carole – Jude hadn't noticed the passage of time), twelve o'clock came round. 'Well, I think we could think about being on our way,' announced Carole.

'Yes, sure.' There was a silence. Jude didn't move from her lounger.

'And we could go and stock up at the supermarket on our way back, rather than leaving the food in a hot car.'

'Mm.' Still no movement, and another silence.

'Well, if we are about to go, perhaps you ought to think about changing your clothes.'

Jude looked down mischievously at her bikini and the rolling curves it failed to control. 'Oh, I thought I could go like this.' Carole's mouth opened, but Jude came in quickly enough to stem the flow of outrage before it started. 'I'll go and change,' she said humbly. And then giggled as she went into the villa.

The incongruous thing about Hisarönü is that it is so close to the well-tended rustic simplicity of Kayaköy. A visitor only had to drive a few miles out of the village and up a pine-forested hillside, but once in Hisarönü they could have been on another planet.

Carole drove, which was what always happened in Fethering. Though Jude could drive, she didn't own a car, so most of their mutual excursions were in Carole's Renault. And it seemed natural for the same pattern to repeat itself with the Fiat Bravo in Turkey.

Knowing from what she'd read in a guidebook that parking in the centre of Hisarönü could be a problem, Carole found an empty space on the outskirts. Having checked for line markings on the road and parking permits in other vehicles, she concluded that they were safe to park there.

They were beside the high rectangular block of a hotel. A board outside advertised its evening entertainments in coloured chalks. Monday: Bingo. Tuesday: Quiz Night. Wednesday: Belly Dancer. Thursday: Country & Western. Friday: Karaoke. Saturday: Barn Dance.

Carole looked at the list with distaste.

'Well, that's Saturday night sorted,' said Jude.

'What do you mean?'

'We'll go to the Barn Dance.'

'What! The idea of going to a Barn Dance under any circumstances is appalling. Going to one in a foreign country where one does not know anyone else is . . .' Her words trickled away as she took in the expression on her friend's face. Carole Seddon was not always very good at recognizing when people were making jokes.

'Hm,' she said and they walked in silence into Hisarönü.

The silence didn't last long. Every step they took revealed more evidence of the way the entire town was geared to the demands of British holidaymakers. And not, to Carole's mind, the nicest kind of British holidaymakers.

Every restaurant they passed offered competitive prices (in Turkish lira or pounds) on full English breakfasts – many with the additional incentive of HP sauce and Tetley tea. Roast Sunday dinners with Yorkshire pudding also featured strongly. There were pubs called the Queen Vic and the Rovers Return. Restaurant names included Rumble-Tums, The Bee's Knees, Robin Hood and Delboy's. The theme of the *Only Fools and Horses* sitcom was continued in a retail outlet called Trotter's Independent Trading Shop. Amongst its goods on offer were bottle openers shaped like penises, along with watches and sunglasses actually advertised as 'Genuine Fake'. It was only one of many shops and stalls selling tourist tat. Between them, hairdressers, nail bars and tattoo parlours abounded. A soundtrack of English 70s pop music blared from every doorway.

Carole Seddon was in a state of perpetual shudder, which was not improved by the sight of the tourists who thronged the streets. As feared, there were a plethora of tattoos and Union Jack T-shirts. Obese women with their hair pulled tightly back into scrunchies had far too much glitter on their eyelids and their denim shorts. Too many for Carole's taste wore nothing more than a bikini. And far too many of the voices she heard came from the Midlands or the North. Which, in Carole Seddon's lexicon, meant they were 'common'.

What made this transplanted British enclave even odder was the number of Turkish elements which still remained. Women in traditional dress of baggy trousers and headscarves swept the pavements in front of the shops. Their menfolk sat around outside cafés smoking and sipping at sweet tea in gilded glasses. Young men with cropped black hair buzzed about on their scooters like lazy insects.

The whole set-up prompted uncomfortable thoughts in Carole. She was against the idea of foreign destinations being converted into outposts of Britain, but equally she never felt quite relaxed when abroad. And she suspected that her reaction against Hisarönü was basically social. What she objected to was the idea of transplanting Blackpool to Turkey. While if the place being transplanted was somewhere more genteel . . . say, Fethering perhaps . . . well, that might be a lot more acceptable. And then she reflected that in some ways Kayaköy was perhaps not a million miles from Fethering transplanted to Turkey.

They couldn't miss the Dirty Duck. The whole frontage of the two-storey building was painted a virulent, almost fluorescent, yellow. The pillars of the vine-covered front terrace were also yellow, and outside hung a pub sign of a cartoon duck looking lasciviously through binoculars at distant bikini-clad girls on a beach. The menus, the mats, the coasters and everything else on which there was room to fit it carried the same logo.

They sat down at one of the terrace tables and were greeted instantly by a bonhomous young man in a Dirty Duck polo shirt. It clearly never occurred to him to address them in anything but English. 'Hello, pretty ladies,' he said. 'Could I get you something to drink?'

Jude opted again for a large Efes. 'It's so refreshing in this heat,' she said, 'but I must stop drinking it soon or I'll just swell up like a balloon.'

Though conscious that she was going to have to drive, Carole reckoned one glass of white wine would be all right.

'A dry one you like, madam? We have very good – it's like a Sauvignon Blanc.'

'Yes, that'll be fine, thank you.'

'Large or small?'

'Large,' Jude answered for her.

While the man went for their drinks, they studied the menu. It was all predictable English pub fare (or 'Pubbe Grubbe' as the menu insisted on calling it). As well as the inevitable full English breakfast, there were fish and chips, steak and ale pie, hunter's chicken, sausage and mash and so on. 'Goodness,' said Carole, 'that all looks so filling.'

'I don't know,' said Jude. 'I'm feeling quite peckish.'

Carole looked into the interior. There, the fierce yellow paint had given way to a dark wood effect with coloured glass lampshades and a perfect replica of an English pub bar. She was hoping to see Donna Lucas, but there was no sign of her. Carole wondered – and indeed worried – about the best way of finding out if she was on the premises.

By the time their drinks arrived, she had, to her relief, found a part of the menu featuring some lighter dishes, and when asked she ordered a cheese omelette. Jude went for the sausage and mash.

'Very good choice,' said the waiter. 'Wall's sausages shipped over specially from England. Not spicy like Turkish sausage.'

'Sounds great,' said Jude. 'Oh, by the way, is Donna Lucas around?'

'Donna? Yes.'

'It's just, we met her briefly at Dalaman Airport, and she said if we came here we'd get special rates.'

'Of course. I'll tell her you are here.'

EIGHTEEN

Jude took a long, blissful sip from her beer. The first sip was always the best, just the sheer coldness on her tongue, the tingle of the bubbles. Thereafter, she knew, would follow a process of diminishing returns as the beer approached room temperature and she became more aware of the blandness of its taste. But it was worth it for that first moment.

'If we do see Donna,' said Carole, 'what are we going to ask her?'

But there was no time to make plans because at that moment the landlady came bouncing out from the bar to greet them. Denim shorts were tight at the top of her chubby legs, and she wore a red T-shirt with a large Dirty Duck logo on the front.

'Carole and Jude, isn't it?' she asked.

'You've got a very good memory,' said Jude, whereas Carole just thought Nita must have discussed them with her friend before they'd appeared at Dalaman Airport.

'Welcome to the Dirty Duck.' She gestured round her domain. 'Mine, all mine.'

'You run it on your own?'

'Yes. I did have a husband who in theory was my partner in the business, but once the hard work started he lost interest. Contrived to lose interest in me at the same time. So now I no longer have a husband and the Dirty Duck's all mine.'

'Was your husband Turkish?' asked Carole.

Donna's brows wrinkled. 'That's an odd thing to ask.'

'Sorry. I just thought, having met Nita's husband . . .'

'Ah, the mighty Erkan.' Though whether she used the adjective as a compliment or in irony was hard to say. 'No, my husband was a Brit. Still is, come to that – just, thank God, no longer my husband. He's still around – though I avoid him like the plague. He's to be seen in the bars of Fethiye, slowing drinking himself to death on raki. Which is fine by me. Thank God we never had any children.'

'Nita hasn't got children either, has she?' asked Jude, steering the conversation in the direction she wanted it to go.

'No. And I think she'd echo my "thank God" for that.'

'How do you mean?'

'This is an extremely male-oriented society out here. Once you're lumbered with kids it's fairly difficult to have much of a life of your own. It's hard enough when you haven't got them. That's why my friendship with Nita's so important to me. It's easier to be independent when there's two of you on the same side.'

Carole was by now sure that Donna had no idea her friend was dead and that it would be a serious blow to her when she did find out. But she wondered whether Donna had also been fed the story about Nita returning to England to tend to her sick mother. 'I actually tried ringing her once or twice yesterday,' Carole lied, 'but she hasn't rung back. Do you know if she's around?'

'I assume so. I haven't heard anything to the contrary.'

Jude now joined the lying bandwagon. 'Actually, the problem might be that she left her mobile at Morning Glory.'

'Did she?' asked an astounded Carole.

'Yes. Well, at least, I assume it was hers. I can't think who else could have left it . . . though maybe it was some earlier tenants at the villa.'

'Well,' said Donna, 'it's easy enough to check if it is hers.'

'Oh?'

'Yes, if you just switch the phone on and go into—'

'Don't we need a passcode to do that?'

'You probably do, yes. Well, there's a very strong chance that passcode would be "1066". I remember once having a conversation with Nita about pins and passwords, and she said the Battle of Hastings was the only date she could remember from history so she used it for everything electronic. I think there's a strong chance that'd be the code for the iPhone.'

'Oh, thank you. Well, we'll try it when we get back to Morning Glory.'

'Yes. Mind you,' said Donna thoughtfully, 'if it actually is Nita's phone it'd be getting lots of calls. Has it been ringing a lot?'

'Not once,' replied Carole.

'Then it probably isn't hers.'

The two investigators exchanged the smallest looks of disappointment.

'Nita's has got a very distinctive case – pale-blue fishes on a dark-blue background.'

Carole and Jude were even more disappointed. They'd got it wrong. The case of the phone they'd picked up at Pinara had the colours the opposite way round; the fishes were dark-blue on a pale-blue background.

'One of the things I know from my days being a courier and tour guide,' Donna went on, 'is that your mobile never stops ringing.'

Jude looked ruefully at Carole. Of course, given where they'd found the phone, they had rather jumped to the conclusion that it must have been Nita's, but now it seemed more likely that someone else had dropped it there. Not surprising, really, with people clambering over rocks and tree trunks; a phone could easily slip out of a pocket or knapsack. So probably the mobile had nothing to do with Nita's death. Strange, though, that the two cases should be so similar.

But even as Jude had this dispiriting thought, another much

more cheering one came into her mind. Maybe, rather than belonging to the victim, the phone had been dropped by her murderer.

Their food arrived – and very nice it looked too. The sausage and mash was indistinguishable from the excellent dish served at the Crown and Anchor in Fethering. Jude wasn't too bothered about their not embracing Turkish culture for one lunch. They'd have lots more local cuisine before they left. Besides, she was hungry.

Carole, meanwhile, having made a start on her omelette (garnished with a container-load of chips) was off on an investigative diversion of her own. For reasons that were not clear to Jude, she told Donna about the painted non-welcome they'd been greeted with on their arrival at Morning Glory.

The landlady of the Dirty Duck was puzzled and echoed almost exactly the words Nita had used when the message had first been discovered. 'Nobody in Kayaköy would have done that – nobody local, anyway. They value the tourist trade too much.'

'Nita seemed pretty sure it wasn't aimed at us.'

'It couldn't have been.'

'So who would it have been aimed at?'

Donna shrugged. 'Barney, perhaps. His business activities round here haven't made him popular with everyone.'

'When we were with Barney at Cin Bal on our first evening . . .'

'Oh, he took you there did he – for an "authentic Turkish experience"?'

'He did. And he was attacked there by a man called Kemal.'

'Ah, yes. Well, he's certainly got his knife into Barney.'

'He almost literally had that night,' said Jude.

'And you're wondering whether Kemal might have been responsible for the welcome graffiti at Morning Glory?'

'Yes. A couple of the words were misspelled.'

'Well, it's a thought. Not impossible – assuming he could see straight enough to paint the words. I'm afraid Kemal has the same problem as my ex – the dreaded booze. So cheap out here.'

It's strange,' said Carole. 'For a Muslim country there does seem to be a lot of alcohol around.'

'Turkey is a very pragmatic Muslim country,' said Donna. 'It's all down to another Kemal. Atatürk. He brought in the Western alphabet, Western weekends, and tolerance of Western habits – including everyone pouring the booze down their throats like there's no tomorrow.'

'Yes, I've read quite a lot about Atatürk,' said Carole. 'An intriguing figure.'

'That's certainly true.'

Jude moved the conversation on. 'How long have you known Nita, Donna?'

The landlady pursed her lips with the effort of memory. 'Phew, must be nearly twenty years – God, it *is* twenty years! We met when we first came out here as travel couriers, hardly out of our teens then. We bonded straight away. It was important to have someone supportive around, someone of the same gender. There was a lot of casual sexism around, so we had to learn to toughen up quite quickly out here. Nita was great to me back then, doing a real big-sister job. I was pretty naive, but she was tougher. Well, she'd had to be. Lost her mother to cancer when she was about twelve, and virtually brought up her younger brothers on her own.'

Carole and Jude exchanged looks. They hadn't been convinced by Barney's story of Nita having to rush back to England because her mother was ill. Now they knew it to be a lie.

'And you've stayed in touch with Nita ever since, have you?' asked Jude.

'Yes. There were long breaks when we didn't see each other. You know, during the winters or when we were posted to different parts of Turkey. But even then we kept in touch – emails, texts, you know.'

'Don't answer this if you don't want to,' Jude began, 'but I got the distinct impression, seeing them together, that there once was something going on between Nita and Barney.'

Donna giggled. 'Don't think that's much of a secret these days. Not sure that it ever was one. Business demands meant that Barney was quite often in Turkey on his own. When he was, he and Nita hooked up straight away. If he came out with his wife, they played it a bit cooler.'

'And, as far as you know, is it still going on?' Jude made a conscious effort to use the present tense. She didn't want Donna to have any suspicion that Nita was no longer alive.

Donna grimaced with uncertainty. 'That I don't know. They certainly keep very closely in touch. But I guess things were different after Nita married Erkan.'

'How long have they been married?'

'Must be getting on for ten years now.'

'I must say,' said Carole, 'that when we saw them together, there didn't seem to be much love lost.'

'No, it isn't exactly a Mills and Boon romance. I think Erkan kind of lost interest when it became clear that Nita wasn't going to produce the son he so wanted. That kind of thing counts for a lot out here.'

'Could Nita just not conceive?' asked Jude.

'No, I think she could,' Donna replied.

'That's rather a strange answer.'

'Yes, I suppose it is. It's just things Nita's said to me at times, you know, when we're on the second bottle of wine. That she might have continued to use contraception . . . Like she didn't want the commitment of having children with Erkan. You know, like I said earlier about my marriage.'

'Are you suggesting,' asked Jude, 'that Nita's still holding a candle for Barney?'

'I suppose it's possible. Her marriage to Erkan always seemed to be more of a commercial transaction than a love match.'

'Oh?'

'When they met he was just a diving instructor for another company. She was keen on scuba diving and had some lessons with him.'

'Did she continue with it?'

'Yes, she was very good.' Donna wrinkled her nose. 'I don't know if you've ever tried it, but it's not for me. I've never fancied it, all that business of putting your head under water. I had one lesson and got terribly claustrophobic. That was enough. But Nita loved scuba diving from the start. And it was Nita's business brain that enabled Erkan to set up his own diving school. Her brain and Barney's money.'

'Really?'

'Yes, Barney bankrolled Erkan when he set up his own diving school. He bought a company that was going belly-up and put a lot of money into making a swish, state-of-the-art enterprise.'

'Was that so Erkan would always be in his debt?'

'Possibly.'

'And Erkan wouldn't be able to complain if Barney continued his relationship with Nita?'

Donna looked at Jude and nodded slowly in admiration. 'Yes, that's what I've wondered more than once. Nita never said it to me in so many words, but she said things – again well into the second bottle of wine – which implied that might be what was going on.'

Donna's openness was very welcome. Jude got the impression that she was as intrigued about her friend as they were, that although she was close to Nita there were still areas of her life to which she had always been denied access.

So she felt empowered to ask her next question. 'Did you know Barney's first wife, Zoë?'

'I wouldn't say "knew" her. I met her a few times.'

'And did she arrive on the scene before Barney had started his relationship with Nita?'

'No. And, needless to say, Nita was pretty miffed about the news. So far as she was concerned, she and Barney were an item – though, of course, she only saw him when his business brought him out to Turkey. What he got up to while he was in England, she had to take on trust.'

Which was probably a rather foolish thing to do, Jude reflected. She thought about the timescale and realized that when she and Barney had their brief affair he was quite possibly already involved with Nita. While it was going on, Jude had never properly trusted Barney. There was always time in his life unaccounted for, time when the demands of his business took him away. Often abroad. Quite frequently to Turkey. She felt even more glad she'd been firm with him when he'd suggested rekindling their relationship.

'And then suddenly,' Donna went on, 'Barney's out in Kayaköy with a brand-new wife. Which, as you can imagine, was a bit of a slap in the face for Nita.'

'I can see that. And was it on that first trip out here that Zoë died?'

'No, it was a couple of years later. Because by then she was quite an experienced diver. Got her OWD.' In response to the blank faces she explained, 'Open Water Diving certificate. That made it even stranger that she had the accident.'

'Do you know exactly how it happened?' asked Jude.

'Not the details, no. Barney and Nita both clammed up about it. Zoë drowned, that's all I know.'

'And when,' asked Carole, 'did Nita and Erkan get married? And, indeed, when did they set up Erkan's business?'

Donna's brow wrinkled with the effort of memory. 'That would be fairly soon after the first time Barney brought Zoë out here.'

'So maybe that was a kind of pay-off to Nita from Barney? "Thank you very much for all your loyal service, now I suggest you marry Erkan and I'll give you the money to set up a business together"?'

'I must say, at the time I wondered if that was what had happened.'

A raucous crowd of English had just entered the Dirty Duck. Large men in shorts and sticklike women with wraps over bikinis. Union Jack T-shirts and far too many tattoos for Carole's taste.

'Hello, Donna darling!' one of the men called out. 'Back again for your daily specials.'

'Be with you in a moment, Bazza love,' she called back, the perfect East End landlady. 'Have to go, girls.'

'And what do we do?' asked Carole, who had just finished her omelette, but only got halfway through the mountain of chips. 'Pay at the bar?'

'No, you don't. These are on me.'

'Oh no, we can't accept—'

'Told you at Dalaman Airport you'd get special rates, didn't I?'

'Yes,' said Jude, 'but there's a difference between special rates and getting our whole lunch on the house.'

'Not at the Dirty Duck there isn't,' said Donna with a grin.

Jude looked at Carole, dissuading her from further argument. 'Well, in that case, we will say a very gracious thank-you for your generosity.'

'My pleasure, love.'

'And look . . .' Jude pulled a scrap of paper out of her bag and scribbled on it. 'Here are our mobile numbers. If you hear anything from Nita, could you ask her if she's lost a phone?'

'Of course. And you've got the number here, haven't you?'

Jude nodded.

'It's strange,' Donna continued. 'I haven't heard from her in the last couple of days. Not even a text – that's unlike Nita.'

Donna Lucas looked worried. And Carole felt bad. She couldn't say anything at that point, but she knew the landlady of the Dirty Duck was due soon to get some very upsetting news.

NINETEEN

'It's a pity we didn't bring the mobile with us,' said Jude as they made their way back to the car. 'Then we could check out the "1066" code. Still, we can do it as soon as we get back to Morning Glory.'

'Yes, except now it seems like the phone has nothing to do with Nita.'

'It's odd, though, that the two cases are so similar, just with the colours reversed. That makes me think there might be some connection. Anyway, we can check back at the villa. If the "1066" code works, then we'll *know* there's a connection.'

'Hm. Of course, we're not going back to Morning Glory straight away,' said Carole firmly.

'Why not?'

'Because we're very near to Ölüdeniz. And Ölüdeniz is where Erkan has his diving school.' She pulled out of her bag

a flyer that she'd picked up in Morning Glory. 'And I think
Erkan has to be our next port of call.'

Jude didn't disagree.

Ölüdeniz was as much targeted at British tourists as Hisarönü,
but in a slightly more tasteful and upmarket way. There were,
to Carole's relief, fewer Union Jack T-shirts and tattoos. It
was very much a regimented seaside resort, pebbly beach laid
out with parallel rows of loungers and umbrellas. Given
how relatively early it was in the season, a surprising number
of the loungers were occupied. Overhead, there was a lot of
paragliding activity.

The directions on the flyer took them straight to Erkan's
diving school. It had a prime position on the sea front and
looked to be very well appointed. Whatever his motives for
making his investment, Barney Willingdon had not stinted on
it. Either side of the large glass doors were blown-up photographs in vivid colours of divers and the marine life they
encountered. Inside, the office area was air conditioned and
the side walls hung with various items which might have meant
something to a diver but didn't to Carole or Jude. Through
the glass doors at the back could be seen a pool, beside which
a deeply tanned instructor was demonstrating scuba equipment
to a small group of tourists in swim shorts and bikinis.

Carole and Jude were greeted as they entered the building
by a very articulate Turkish girl in blue shorts and a white
polo shirt with the school's logo on it. 'Welcome,' she said in
a voice which suggested she'd learned her English from
Americans, 'to the best diving company in the Fethiye area.
Have you ever dived before?'

'Well, no, though actually what we—'

But Carole was not allowed to complete her explanation.
'We do very good course for beginners. Very cheap, one day
only. You get introductory lesson on the basics of diving, then
sea dive in small groups with instructor and—'

Jude tried to interrupt the flow. 'Yes, all we really want
to—'

'Then there is a two-day course. You learn obviously much
more in this. There are three sessions of knowledge development,

three dives in confined water and two in open water. And this gives you a qualification in—'

'We're really looking for Erkan.'

'Yes, Erkan is boss here. This is Erkan's school. Very good school, very high standards, particularly good safety record. All advanced divers go out with a buddy, all equipment is checked and rechecked and—'

'We actually,' Carole crashed in, 'want to speak to Erkan!'

This did stop the girl in her tracks. But only for a moment. 'Speak to Erkan? There is no need. You can book a course by me. You do not have to deal with Erkan.'

'No, we want to talk to him about something else.'

'Something else?'

'Something not to do with diving.'

The girl looked shocked. 'Not to do with diving?'

'No.'

Her manner changed completely now she realized that her sales pitch had been falling on deaf ears. 'Erkan is not here today,' she said abruptly.

'Do you know when he's likely to be back?'

'No.'

And that was it, really. The girl made it pretty clear that they were not welcome in her office any more. They thanked her and made for the exit.

But when they got there, the doors were held open for them. And Jude recognized the person who held them open as Fergus McNally. Carole couldn't have provided a name, but she also recognized him – as the man she'd seen in Fethiye with Henry Willingdon.

Fergus had also been hoping to speak to Erkan, and when Jude told him that the diving school's owner wasn't there, he readily acceded to her suggestion that they should have a drink. So they sat on the shaded terrace of a steel and glass seafront café/bar. At an adjacent table, a group of young Englishmen in brightly patterned swim shorts tried to outdo each other with tales of their paragliding exploits.

Carole, aware of her driving duties and the wine she'd had at the Dirty Duck, ordered a double espresso. The other two had large beers. Jude's worries about putting on weight still weren't strong enough to defeat the temptation of that beautiful condensation-dripping mug.

'Well, this is a surprise,' said Jude. 'When we met in the Crown and Anchor, you didn't say you were going to come out here.'

'I didn't know I was going to come out here then.'

'So, what, is this just a last-minute holiday?' asked Carole.

'Hardly. I am not, sadly, in a position where I can take last-minute holidays. Or holidays of any kind, come to that. No, I'm here because I was asked to come out here.'

'By Barney Willingdon?' Jude suggested.

'No. No way. It's a long time since I've been at Barney's beck and call.'

'So who asked you?'

'Henry Willingdon.'

'Yes, I knew she was out here,' said Carole.

Fergus looked shocked. 'How?'

And she told him of her sighting of them in Fethiye.

'That's where we're staying. In a hotel there. Hotel Osman.'

'Does Barney know you're here?' asked Jude.

'No, and he mustn't know either. It was Henry's idea. She wanted to come out here, and she wanted to be with someone who was familiar with the territory. And, as I told you, I'd been out a few times with Barney back in the early days.'

'So Henry stumped up for your flight?'

'Yes. And she's paying me too.'

'What is she paying you for, exactly?' asked Carole.

'That's between us. A business arrangement.'

It was clear from the jut of his chin that they wouldn't get any more information on that subject. But Jude still tried. 'Is it something to do with Barney or Barney's business affairs?'

'Sorry, I can't tell you that. I'm being paid for my discretion, apart from anything else.'

Carole nodded. 'Fine. But it wasn't pure coincidence that we met you at the diving school. You said you wanted to talk to Erkan.'

'So?'

'Well, we wanted to talk to him too.'

'I don't see what relevance that has.'

'It could be relevant if we both wanted to see Erkan for the same reason.'

'Like what?'

'We're quite interested in finding out exactly what happened to Barney's first wife, Zoë.'

'Really?'

'And we were wondering whether you might be following the same investigative route.'

'Well, I'm not,' he said with a finality which made both women certain he was lying. They felt sure he was being paid by Henry Willingdon to find out more about her predecessor's death.

Carole tried another tack. 'Presumably, you know Erkan's wife, Nita?'

'Yes.'

'When did you first meet her?'

'First time I came out here with Barney.'

'Were the two of you in partnership at that point?'

'No, he brought me out here because he'd got a couple of projects that needed investment. Thought I might be interested.'

'And did you invest?'

'Not then, no. Look, I told you all this, Jude.'

'Yes, but Carole hasn't heard it. You said you didn't invest in Barney's projects out here.'

'No, had cash flow problems. Not too bad, but I couldn't rustle up the kind of sums he was talking about; not at short notice, anyway. No, I'd have done all right if I'd gone in with Barney at that point.'

'Rather than waiting till you got involved in his Northern Cyprus project?' Jude prompted.

'Yes. I think if I'd gone in with Barney earlier I might not have got so comprehensively stuffed.'

'Going back to Nita . . .' said Carole.

'Uh-huh.'

'We've heard rumours that Barney and she had had some fling back then.'

'And how! They were all over each other. We're talking

quite a while back here. Barney was thirty, I suppose, and Nita hardly out of her teens. She was stunning then. Long time since I've seen her, so I don't know what she looks like now.'

Carole, unfortunately, knew all too well what Nita looked like now, but she wasn't about to share the information.

'So the two of them were an item?'

'Very definitely, yes. I mean, they weren't often seen out together – they were discreet up to a point. The travel companies don't like their tour guides to have boyfriends too openly – can upset the punters, many of whom cast lecherous eyes on the girls and don't want their fantasies ruined. But evenings after Nita had knocked off from work . . . yes, they were very definitely an item.'

'And this was before Barney got married to Zoë?'

'Oh yes. Barney was a bit of a Jack the lad back then. Kept quite a few women on a string, so far as I can gather.' Yes, he did, thought Jude ruefully. 'But out here it was just him and Nita.'

'So,' said Carole, 'she must have been pretty put out when he suddenly announced he was marrying Zoë?'

'I would assume so. I wasn't here when that news broke.' His face darkened. 'That's when I was starting to get involved in Barney's projects in Northern Cyprus.'

'One thing . . .' Jude began. 'You said Barney wasn't to know that you're in Turkey. Presumably, he knows that Henry's here?'

'No,' Fergus replied with some force. 'And she very much doesn't want him to.'

'That's not going to be easy, is it?' asked Carole. 'With her only being in Fethiye, and Barney seeming to be best mates with everyone in the area. We're very quickly discovering that there are no secrets in Kayaköy.'

'Henry's staying in the hotel most of the time. She wants to choose for herself the moment when she makes contact with Barney.'

'When she confronts him?' suggested Carole.

'I didn't use that word.' Fergus McNally was becoming very guarded.

'When,' intuited Jude, 'you've reported back to her on how her predecessor, Zoë, died?'

But he wasn't going to be drawn on that either. Something one of them had said had made him clam up. They exchanged mobile numbers, and no one suggested staying for a second drink.

TWENTY

On the way back from Ölüdeniz they stopped at the Kayaköy supermarket to load up with essentials. And to Carole's mind, seeing the amount of wine and beer Jude loaded into their basket, some non-essentials too. They were served this time by a smiling woman, presumably the wife of the owner, wearing traditional baggy trousers and headscarf. But she, too, knew both their names and the fact that they were staying at Morning Glory.

As soon as they were back there, Jude pounced on the drawer where they had left the iPhone found at Pinara. 'Funny, isn't it? The two phone cases with reversed colours. It does suggest to me that they might be owned by the same person.'

'Well, we'll know that's true if "1066" works, won't we?'

Jude tried switching the phone on, and an expression of predictable disgust came across her face. 'Out of bloody power. How is it that they can get so much battery life on a tablet and still so little on a phone?'

'Don't worry,' said Carole, feeling suddenly empowered by her prescience. Serenely moving towards the stairs, she announced, 'I have a "universal all-in-one mobile phone charger". And an adaptor for Turkish sockets.'

'Ooh, get you,' said Jude, half under her breath. 'Think of everything.'

Carole plugged the lead into the adaptor and then, with a bit of hard pushing, the adaptor into the socket. She switched the iPhone on. It immediately told her that the charger she

was using was not the official Apple product and might not
be supported.

But it was. The home screen appeared and, as instructed,
she slid to unlock. A grid of ten numbers appeared. Tensely,
she entered '1066'.

It worked.

'Brilliant,' said Jude. 'So it did belong to Nita!'

But accessing the phone only worked in the sense that a
new screen opened up. It showed a weather forecast for Fethiye.
How to move from that to some other function, Carole did
not have a clue. Rather disappointed that she couldn't complete
the revelation, she reluctantly asked Jude if she had any idea
about the interior workings of an iPhone.

'I've got a friend with an iPad, and I think the basics are
much the same.' She took the mobile from Carole and pressed
the indented white square at the bottom of the screen.
Immediately, a grid of different icons appeared. 'Let's try the
phone first – see if there are any messages, or at least a list
of recent callers.'

Jude showed sufficient dexterity with the options to get
where she wanted to. She checked the screen. 'Well, that's
very odd.'

'What's very odd?' asked Carole, a little tetchy at having
become the sidekick in this part of the investigation. Since
finally coming round to computers, she had always rather
prided herself on her technological know-how.

'No voicemails. And no record of any recent calls.' Jude
touched the screen a few more times. 'And only one number
in the contacts list.'

'What does that suggest?'

'Well, either that the owner had very few friends . . . or
that she – or perhaps he – had only recently got the phone
and hadn't got round to putting in their contacts list.'

'But the one contact that *is* there, Jude – is that name
significant? One you recognize?'

'It's just a single letter.'

'"B"?' asked Carole excitedly.

'That'd be too much to hope for. No, it's "L".'

'Most peculiar.'

'Yes.'

'Isn't there anything else we can try?'

'Texts – maybe they sent each other texts?' Jude's fingers worked away on the screen, and a smile of satisfaction appeared on her well-rounded face. 'Yes, much more promising.'

She showed her findings to Carole. The last text received on the iPhone read: 'See you tomorrow 11 am. Old place. Old purpose. Let's recapture the moment. L'

The text was dated two days before. The Monday, the day Carole and Jude had arrived in Kayaköy. And the day before Carole had found Nita's body.

Were they jumping to conclusions to think that 'the old place' could be the tomb at Pinara? And that the text was setting up an assignation between Nita and someone else? But who? The obvious candidate for the job would be Barney. But so far they had nothing except circumstance to connect the text message to him.

'I reckon this must have been a dedicated phone,' said Jude.

'What do you mean?'

'A phone line only used by two people. That's why there's only the one contact in it. If it rings then the other person immediately knows who's calling and can answer or not according to what circumstances or company they are in. It's quite a popular cover method used by people having an affair.'

'Is it?' Carole sniffed. 'I wouldn't know about that.'

'Well, there's one thing we can try to see if the other person is Barney.' As she spoke, Jude deftly pressed the screen to make the call. She could hear the ringing tone from the other end, but no one picked up. Nor did the answering service click in.

'Well, he wouldn't answer, would be?' said Carole.

'Why not?'

'Because he told us that thing about Nita having been called away to England because her mother's ill. We now know her mother died when she was twelve, which must mean Barney knew Nita was dead. So he knows it can't be her making the call.'

'Possibly, but not necessarily.'

'I can't see any alternative.'

'The alternative possibility is that Barney was merely reporting what he had been told. That someone else told him Nita had gone to England.'

'I suppose it's just possible,' Carole said grudgingly. 'But unlikely . . . I mean, they'd had this long relationship . . . surely, at some point Nita would have mentioned her mother's early death?'

'Who knows?' asked Jude in a manner Carole didn't find helpful. 'Still,' she went on, 'perhaps they never used the dedicated mobile for phoning – that's why there's no record of recent calls. Perhaps they only used it for texting.'

'Hm,' mumbled Carole, unwilling to admit that this was actually quite a good idea. 'So what do we do now?'

'I don't think we can put it off any longer. We contact Barney.'

'What, text him on this phone?'

'No, he'll smell a rat if we do that. I'll just call him on his mobile.'

'Do you want to do that on your own?'

'Why should I?' But Jude could feel herself blushing. She didn't think she could keep from Carole's beady scrutiny that there was a history between her and Barney Willingdon for much longer.

So she made the call right there in the main room of Morning Glory. And there was no reply from Barney's mobile.

Though it was only the previous evening that they'd seen him at Antik, Jude still got the feeling that he was deliberately not picking up the phone. She left him a message, though without much hope of its being returned.

Every possible advance they could make on their investigation seemed to involve talking to Barney. And both of them wanted very much to get on with the investigation.

Jude stripped down to a bikini and lay on a lounger, but was still clearly distracted. She couldn't get comfortable and kept moving towels and shifting her position. Her trashy novel was unable to reassert its tenuous hold on her attention. Eventually, she said, 'There is one person we could ask where Barney might be.'

'Who? And don't say "Erkan" because we've—'

'Not Erkan. Our neighbour.'

'You mean,' said Carole with an involuntary shudder, 'Travers Hughes-Swann.'

'Yes. He said he'd watched Barney building every one of his villas. He might well know which one he's likely to be in.'

Carole harrumphed but was forced to admit Travers was their only lead. She looked disapprovingly at her friend's bikini décolletage. 'If we go and see him, I hope you're going to be wearing rather more than that.'

'You bet I am,' came the reply. 'I've heard of roving eyes. His eyes don't rove, they remain firmly fixed on the point between the breasts.'

Both of them were wearing high-necked cotton tops as they walked down the track towards Brighton House. As they turned off the track towards the open railed gates, Travers Hughes-Swann stepped forward from the house to greet them. 'Well, hello. How very nice to see you lovely ladies. And you've timed it very well; I've just put the kettle on.'

His words again gave them the uncomfortable feeling that they had been spied on, that he had heard them planning the visit and put the kettle on in anticipation of their arrival. Though both knew they were probably being paranoid.

Travers was dressed as he had been when each of them had met him, in khaki shorts and thick leather sandals over beige woollen socks. With an expansive gesture which somehow didn't suit him, he said, 'Welcome to Brighton House!'

Jude was intrigued to see the building he had so vaunted over Morning Glory, and her first impressions were not great. Travers's idea of keeping the authenticity of Turkish tradition seemed to involve the minimum of modernization. He'd said that Brighton House had been converted from old farm buildings, and that was exactly what they still looked like. A low-pitched roof of red clay tiles seemed to be the only improvement he had made. If he'd perhaps aimed to create rustic charm, then all he had achieved was an aura of scruffiness.

But if he had done little to adapt the house itself, he'd clearly focused his building ambitions on the garden. With, in the view of both women, mixed success. If this was what

Travers Hughes-Swann reckoned to be traditional Turkish style, then he'd read different guidebooks from Carole's.

Certainly, he'd used the authentic local stone, but what he'd done with it was more in keeping with an eighteenth-century Gothic folly than a Turkish garden. The rockeries were kind of all right – it was hard to go wrong with the resplendent plant life available in Turkey – but even they had a rather dated fifties feel. The other structures, however, were the worst kind of garden-centre kitsch – elaborate water-features, point-less grottoes, free-standing unfinished walls. And, to compound the tastelessness, set into the hillside was a kind of stone arbour, inexpertly modelled on a Lycian tomb.

Given Travers's apparent pride in it, his garden was surpris-ingly ill-tended. Though some of the plants were neatly fixed to bamboos with plastic ties, weeds flourished amid the shrubs and flowers. The hedges were shaggy. Wheelbarrows and the apparatus for mixing cement lay untidily on the paths. An ancient battered Land Rover stood on the drive.

One mild surprise was the absence of a pool, which showed the villa was somewhere to live in, rather than to be let out to well-heeled tourists.

Carole and Jude would rather not have been forced to comment on what they saw, but Travers Hughes-Swann's next words, 'Well, what do you think of it?' rather cut off that escape route.

'Well,' said Jude. 'It must've taken hours.'

'Certainly did,' he replied with satisfaction.

'And did you do it all on your own?' asked Carole.

'Oh yes. All my own work. I don't believe in paying people to execute work which has all been my own conception. I'm not like your mate Barney.'

'Talking of our mate Barney—'

'But, as I say, the kettle's on. Now what would you like – tea or coffee? Or,' he asked suspiciously, 'are you the kind of English tourists who spend all your time in foreign countries knocking back the cheap booze?'

'Certainly not,' said Carole, and Jude, who would quite have fancied a beer or a glass of wine, mumbled some similar sentiment. Both agreed that coffee would be nice – Jude's with milk, Carole's without.

'Good. I'm not a drinker myself. I don't like anything that makes me feel out of control. It's lack of control, you know, that makes today's youngsters behave so appallingly. Their parents spent more time trying to *understand* them than discipline them. Since the last war, England has lost its backbone, you know . . .' He must have read something in the women's faces that made him cut short his diatribe. 'Right, well, you just relax in my little suntrap—' he gestured up towards his faux-tomb – 'and I'll sort out the beverages.'

The 'suntrap' was the tidiest part of the garden. No weeds grew between the square stones of its floor, and a broom propped against the wall suggested that it had been recently swept. The idea that Travers might have done it in anticipation of their arrival was slightly unsettling.

Carole and Jude exchanged looks but, feeling that their host might be eavesdropping, didn't say anything. They just sat, slightly awkwardly, on the hard metal chairs in the tomb-like structure, waiting for him to reappear with the tray of coffee.

The mugs which he brought out were chipped and didn't look very hygienic, but it wasn't the moment to comment. Instead, Carole asked, 'And you say your wife is bedridden?'

'Yes, very sad. Totally immobilized by a stroke some years back.'

Jude thought this was rather odd. The previous day Travers had spoken of going out for lunch near Pinara with Phyllis and implied that a sudden deterioration in her condition had made him change his plans. But if his wife was permanently bedridden, then he had just used her as an excuse to ask Jude out for lunch. Which didn't endear him to her.

'I'm sorry to hear that,' said Carole. 'And do you do all the caring yourself?'

'Oh yes. I wouldn't want anyone else involved. You know, I like to feel Phyllis still has her dignity.'

'Of course.'

'Actually, the reason we dropped by,' said Jude, 'is that we wanted to contact Barney, and he doesn't seem to be answering his phone.'

'Oh? Well, why don't you contact Nita? She'll know where he is, for sure.'

Carole didn't want to explain why they didn't try to contact Nita, so she just said, 'She doesn't seem to be answering her phone either.'

'But, Travers,' said Jude, 'you told me you knew all the villas Barney's built round here. I wondered if you might know which one he's likely to be staying in.'

'Well, he doesn't really have a pattern about that. It depends which one's empty . . . you know, hasn't got any holidaymakers in it.'

'Ah, I see.' Jude felt a little dejected. Were they back to the position of waiting until Barney chose to contact them?

'For choice he usually stays in Morning Glory, but of course he won't be doing that with you there.'

'No.'

'As a matter of fact, though, I do happen to know which of his other villas are occupied at the moment.' He winked one wrinkle-surrounded eye. 'I like to keep my ear to the ground, you know. With the right contacts, you can find out everything that goes on in Kayaköy.'

'I'm sure you can.'

'And I'd put money on the fact that Barney's staying in a villa called Tulip Cottage.'

'Oh well, we might drive down and see if Barney's in,' said Carole. 'Where is the villa exactly?'

'Just further along the hillside towards the village. You don't need to take the car. It's easily walkable.'

'Well, thank you.' Jude downed the contents of her coffee mug, trying to avoid the chip on its rim. 'No time like the present. We'll go and see if he's in.'

They both left Brighton House with some relief.

The security at Tulip Cottage was at a considerably higher level than at Morning Glory. Solid metal gates were the only break in a high stone wall surrounding the property. Set in cement to either side of the gates were old clay amphorae. Carole and Jude could not see any of the villa itself except for the terracotta-coloured tiles of its roof.

There was an entryphone with a keypad by the side of the gates. But pressing the call button elicited no response.

TWENTY-ONE

When they got back to Morning Glory, they found they had a visitor. Though they had shut up the villa itself, the main gates were not locked, and sitting on a lounger by the pool was Kemal. He still looked scruffy in jeans and grubby T-shirt, but when he began to speak he was a lot more coherent than when they had last seen him at Cin Bal.

'I thought if I wait you come back here,' he said.

'I was just about to get us a drink,' said Jude as she went across to unlock the front door. 'Can I get you something?'

He shook his head firmly. 'No, today I do not drink.'

'Fine. Not even something non-alcoholic?'

'No.'

'You like a glass of white wine, Carole?'

'That would be very nice.'

Carole sat rather than lounged on another lounger, and there was silence until Jude reappeared with the drinks and asked, 'Well, Kemal, is there something we can do for you?'

'It is more what I can do for you. There is something I can tell you.'

'Oh?'

'I meet the Englishman Fergus this afternoon.'

'Ah, yes, so did we.'

'I know this. He says he sees you. And he says you want to know the same thing he does.'

'Which thing are you talking about?' asked Carole.

'You want to know what happened to Barney Willingdon's first wife.'

Carole and Jude exchanged looks and sat forward. 'Yes, we had wondered,' said Jude.

'I can tell you.'

'It was something to do with a scuba diving accident, wasn't it?'

'It was, yes. It happened at my diving school.'

'Oh, I didn't know you had a diving school too.'

'No, it is same one. It was my diving school. Then business is bad, Barney buys it from me at very cheap price and puts lots of money in for Erkan. He could have invested money for me still to run the school. But, no, he take away my livelihood. Then he spread bad rumours about me, so that I can no longer get work as a diving instructor in the Fethiye area.'

'And you want revenge on him for that? That's why you attacked him at Cin Bal?'

'Yes, but then I was stupid.' He shook his head, as if trying to shake out the memory. 'I was drunk then. I was drunk when I paint message on wall in there.' He nodded towards the villa.

'Ah, that was you, was it? You painted our little welcoming message, did you?'

'It not for you. I think Barney stay here. It for him, to show I have not forgotten, to show I still look for revenge. But that was foolish. Then I was drunk. Today I am not drunk.'

'But you still want revenge on Barney?'

'Proper revenge I want. Revenge through courts. I want him imprisoned for things he has done.'

'And is that why you're telling us what you know?'

'More people know the truth, more he is likely to be arrested. Police will not listen to me. They think me lazy layabout, drunkard. They more likely listen to people like you.'

'Very well then,' said Jude. 'Tell us what happened to Barney's first wife.'

'She very keen on scuba diving. You know about scuba diving?'

'Virtually nothing.'

'Well, is not important the details. All you have to know is that safety is most important. People who learn start with practical demonstration of equipment before they go near water, then in pool, then in sea. And there are certificates people have to get before they go to different levels of diving. Zoë Willingdon does very well at it. First time she come out here with Barney she do beginners' course, then other times she do more and more. She get Advanced Open Water qualification – that means she can dive almost anywhere. She very good.

'Well, there is popular place for advanced divers called Sariyerler. It is like a bay and you can only get there by boat. About one hour from Fethiye harbour. The diving spot is called Three Tunnels, like a reef, though not much coral. A hill in the sea, with the tunnels in it. One side is quite deep, maybe forty-five metres, maybe sixty. Only for very experienced divers, but Zoë has the qualification, she is all right to dive there.

'Anyway, one day she goes out to Sariyerler. I am with her, I drive the boat, and I check all the equipment before she dives. This is very important. You check the first stage, the second stage, the octopus . . . these are technical terms you do not need to know about. And you also check the weight belt.'

'Sorry, what's that?' asked Jude.

'Always for scuba diving you have a weight belt. Living human bodies naturally float, so you need the weight belt to keep you from coming up to the surface. The amount of weight on the belt has to be adjusted to the size of the person, obviously. Some weight belts have pouches which are filled up with lead shot; others use solid weights which are threaded on to the belt. I prefer to use those. And the weight belt has a very secure clasp, so that it cannot come undone by mistake.'

'What would happen if it did come undone by mistake?' asked Carole.

'That would depend on how deep the diver was. Near the surface it would not be much of a problem – you just might have lost the weight belt, that is all. But the deeper you are diving, the more dangerous it becomes. If you are, say, thirty metres down and the weight belt comes off, you start to rise slowly but very quickly accelerate. This is very bad. At thirty metres you are breathing four times atmospheric pressure, so four times as much air as you would on the surface. If you rise very quickly this air expands and will probably burst your lungs. It will kill you, anyway.'

There was a silence. 'And is that what happened to Zoë?' asked Jude.

Kemal nodded. 'I swear I checked the clasp on her weight belt, but somehow it came undone.'

'Accidentally?'

'I don't see how it could be accidental.'

'So someone tampered with it?'

'I think. Tampered – or just undid the clasp. They have a quick-release mechanism for emergencies.'

'And you think it was Barney who undid it?'

'No, Barney was not with us on the boat that day. But I think Barney planned it.'

'Zoë couldn't have done it herself, could she?' asked Carole.

'Suicide? I don't think so. It's a pretty nasty way to go. Anyway, however experienced they are, nobody ever dives alone. You always dive with a "buddy", so the two of you can keep an eye on each other, help out if one or other of you gets into difficulties.'

'Or, in this case, help the other one to get into difficulties by undoing the weight belt?'

'That's what I reckoned, yes. Though it's very difficult to prove.'

'I'm sure it is.'

It was Carole who asked the inevitable question. 'So who was Zoë's "buddy" that day?'

Kemal replied, 'Nita.'

TWENTY-TWO

There was a long silence, then Kemal said, 'Of course, I had no proof that was what happened. When Nita came to the surface – quite a long time after because she came up gradually, as you should from that kind of depth – she claimed she was nowhere near Zoë when the accident happened. She said it was a few moments before she even realized that Zoë wasn't with her.

'And when Barney heard about it, he just wanted the whole thing hushed up – his wife had died in a tragic accident, that was all. Somehow he managed to limit the amount of official investigation there was out here, and he had her body flown back to England for the funeral. But, although he seemed to want to keep it quiet, he still managed to spread around the fact that the accident happened on my watch, so people thought my diving school was not safe. The bookings fell disastrously – that was why Barney could buy the business so cheaply from me. This is why I hate him,' Kemal concluded simply.

'And you think,' asked Carole, 'that Barney set up Nita to sabotage the weight belt?'

'Yes.'

'You don't think she did it off her own bat?'

'Sorry? What does this mean – "bat"?'

'It's just an expression. It means – did she do it herself rather than following Barney's orders?'

'Why should she do that?'

'She had been having a relationship with him. Suddenly, he's introducing a new wife. Nita can't have been very pleased about that.'

'No.' Kemal looked as though he hadn't considered this possibility before. But he quickly dismissed it. 'No, it is something Barney would arrange. It is not something Nita would do . . . from her own bat?'

'Have you seen Nita recently?' asked Jude suddenly.

'No. Not since that evening at Cin Bal.'

'Kemal,' said Carole, 'you mentioned earlier that you wanted to see Barney in prison . . .'

'Yes.'

'For the murder of Zoë?'

The man shrugged. 'Yes. Or for another of his crimes. There are many people he has injured. I do not mind why he is imprisoned; I want revenge.'

'But why didn't you go to the police at the time, when Zoë died?'

'I did not want to draw attention to what might be seen as a lapse in my safety procedures at the diving school. Besides, then Barney was my friend. We were partners in building projects. He wanted his wife's death hushed up; it suited me too that it should be hushed up.'

'And what's made you change your mind about that?'

He spread his hands wide in a gesture of hopelessness. 'Now

I have nothing to lose. My business is gone, my marriage is gone, my reputation is gone. All I now live for is to get revenge on Barney Willingdon.'

There was a silence, then Carole said, 'Earlier you told us that Fergus McNally also wanted to know what happened to Zoë.'

'Yes.'

'He's another man who feels Barney's done the dirty on him.'

'I know this. There are many people who Barney has . . . how do you say it? "Shafted"?'

'Something like that. But do you think Fergus wants to know how she died for the same reason as you do – to get Barney arrested for the crime?'

'No, I don't think that is his reason. He is trying to find out on behalf of another person.'

'Who? Henry, Barney's current wife?'

Kemal nodded. 'Yes, it is she who wants to find out the truth.'

The two women exchanged a quick look before Carole asked, 'Any idea why?'

'I think perhaps she is worried that a man who could arrange to have his first wife killed might consider doing the same for his second.'

All investigative routes seemed to lead to Barney Willingdon. After Kemal had left, they tried phoning him again. But this time his mobile was switched off, not even offering to take a message.

In spite of their large lunch at the Dirty Duck, both women were feeling hungry by then, so Carole offered only token resistance to Jude's proposal that they should eat out again. They didn't take the car but walked out into the thyme-scented evening and found their footsteps leading them back towards the ghost town. And, in spite of the array of other restaurants they passed, eating once more at the Antik seemed a pleasantly easy option. After all, that was where Barney had come looking for them the evening before.

But there was no sign of him that night.

They found the Antik almost empty, but the number of the owner's family who were around made the atmosphere congenial and welcoming. Carole and Jude were subdued, though, both frustrated by their lack of progress on the investigation.

'I almost wish I'd dreamt what I saw in that tomb in Pinara,' said Carole grumpily. 'Wouldn't that be nice – just the fantasy of a middle-aged woman with an overactive imagination? But no, sadly, my mind was not playing tricks. There is absolutely no doubt that I saw Nita and that she'd been strangled. Which is extremely unfortunate and just raises a whole lot of questions. Not only who killed her, but why she had been killed in the tomb at Pinara. And who moved her body? And where is it now?'

'Yes.' Jude paused. There was something she had been keeping from Carole since the idea of their Turkish holiday first came up. She had put off telling her friend for very good reasons, but she felt the moment of revelation could not be deferred much longer.

'I think,' she began cautiously, 'that I can possibly explain why Nita's body was in the tomb.'

'Can you? Well, why on earth haven't you told me before?'

'Because I wasn't sure,' Jude lied. 'But now, taken in conjunction with the text on Nita's phone . . .'

'What do you mean?'

'The message talked about using the old place for the old purpose. And if it came from Barney—'

'Which it seems very likely it did.'

'Well, if it did, it would be in character for him.'

'In what way?'

'I don't think there's much doubt that what was being proposed was a sexual encounter.'

'Oh?'

'And clearly in a place that he and Nita had used for sexual encounters before.'

Carole looked really puzzled. 'But who on earth would want to make love in an ancient monument?'

'Barney would.'

'Really?'

'Yes, he always had a kind of . . . I don't know what you'd call it – a fetish, maybe – for making love in the open air.'

'Oh?' said Carole.

'And the more bizarre the location, the more he liked it. Something about the situation turned him on . . . particularly if it was a kind of public place, where there was a risk of discovery. That always added something to the experience for him.'

There was a long silence before the inevitable question arose. 'And how do you know this, Jude?'

No way round it now. 'Because, a long time ago, I had an affair with Barney.'

'Did you? But you told me you didn't.'

'I didn't exactly say that.'

'You definitely implied that you hadn't had a relationship with him.'

'Well, yes, I thought it was probably simpler if I—'

'This does change things very considerably,' said Carole, in the manner of a hanging judge.

'Only a little, really,' said Jude uncomfortably.

'I mean, if he was just a friend who had chosen to lend you his villa in Turkey, that's one thing. If he's a lover, the situation becomes very different.'

'An *ex*-lover, Carole. From a very long time ago.'

'But it puts me in a very difficult position.'

'Why?'

'Well, if I'm benefiting from what I took to be Barney Willingdon's altruistic generosity and it turns out he's doing it "for services rendered" . . .'

Jude had a horrible conviction that she knew how the sentence would be completed – and she was right.

'Well, it's as if I'm living off immoral earnings.'

Jude's inability completely to suppress a giggle when the line was finally spoken did not improve the atmosphere between them.

'If you'd told me about this before, Jude, I would never have agreed to come to Turkey.'

'I know. That's why I didn't tell you.'

'And you're sure the affair's over?'

'God, yes. Years ago.'

'And neither of you thought you might rekindle it while you were out here?'

Jude couldn't lie in response to the direct question. 'Barney did imply he'd like us to start it up again.'

'Did he?'

'But I made it very clear to him that I wasn't interested.'

'And is that true?'

'Of course it's true. We had a good time, but as I say, it was long ago. Barney always liked sex and he was good at it, but I've never believed in going back over a route I've travelled before.'

'Hm.' Carole took off her glasses, which didn't need polishing, and polished them. 'Well, I can't say I'm happy about the situation.'

'No. I didn't expect you to be.'

'Particularly if Barney turns out to be a double murderer.'

'We must find out whether he is or not,' said Jude, hoping that getting back to their investigation might dilute her friend's disapproval.

'That's going to be difficult if we can't find him. We seem to have run out of avenues of enquiry.'

'I wouldn't say that.'

'What do you mean?'

'There is one avenue of enquiry we haven't explored yet.'

'And what's that?' asked Carole, still grumpy.

'Henry Willingdon. I think tomorrow morning we should go to the Hotel Osman in Fethiye.'

Carole agreed that was worth trying. There was a long silence between them. Then Carole asked, 'And are you saying that when you were in a relationship with Barney Willingdon, you and he used to . . . have sexual encounters in public places?'

'We did a bit,' a blushing Jude admitted. 'Not very often. And we were very young.'

'Hm.' Another long silence. 'And where was the most public . . . or unusual place that you . . . used?'

'The top of a Number twenty-seven bus.'

'Good heavens,' said Carole Seddon.

TWENTY-THREE

They arrived mid-morning. The Hotel Osman was set a little way from the sea at Fethiye, with a view over the marina. Rows and rows of yachts were moored along the pontoons, and as Carole and Jude moved from the car to the hotel foyer they could hear the clattering of halyards against metal poles.

The Osman was a small hotel, probably family owned. The urbane gentleman behind the reception desk confirmed that Mrs Willingdon and Mr McNally did both have rooms booked in the hotel, but regretted that Mr McNally had left early that morning in the car. Mrs Willingdon, however, was in her room. If they liked to give their names he would ring through to her.

A short telephone conversation ensued, and then Carole and Jude were told that Mrs Willingdon would meet them on the roof terrace. Would they like some tea or coffee sent up? Both opted for coffee and were then directed to the lift and told to go up to the sixth floor.

The roof terrace was well-appointed and high enough above the city to command splendid views to the sea in front and the forest-clad hills behind. It had a small pool with loungers around it and a shaded area with metal table and chairs near an empty bar.

There was no one there when Carole and Jude arrived, so they took seats in the shade and waited. It was not long till Henry Willingdon appeared. She was wearing white cotton trousers and a light-blue top. They remembered her from Chantry House as a rather pale blonde, and she still looked that way, though possibly even paler. Whatever she had been doing since she arrived in Fethiye, it had not involved spending any time in the sun.

The other striking thing about her was that she seemed to be very nervous, almost fearful.

They had only just got through the pleasantries of 'good mornings' when they were interrupted by the arrival of a smiling girl with a tray of two coffees. Henry was asked if she wanted any, but demurred, saying only that she had just had some with her breakfast.

She waited till the girl was safely in the lift before saying, 'This has worked out very well because I wanted to see you two. Fergus was going to drive me out to Kayaköy this afternoon. You do know who I mean by Fergus, don't you?'

'I'd met him back in England,' said Jude, 'and then we both talked to him yesterday in Ölüdeniz.'

'Yes, of course, he told me he'd seen you.'

There was a silence. Henry was evidently not finding the conversation easy, so Jude tried to help out. 'When we saw you at Chantry House the other week, you said you weren't going to come out to Kayaköy with Barney. What made you change your mind?'

'Well, I think the important thing is that I'm not out here *with* Barney. I hope he doesn't even know I'm here.'

'He certainly didn't mention it when we last saw him.'

'And when was that?'

Carole and Jude both did mental calculations, then Carole admitted they hadn't actually seen him since the Tuesday night at Antik.

'And what did he say then?'

'He was just asking us how we were enjoying our stay,' Jude replied.

'And he also told us that Nita had had to go back to England because her mother was ill.' Carole just floated the information to see what reaction it would get. She wasn't about to tell Henry that Nita's mother had died when she was twelve.

'I see.' Henry was still struggling. 'The reason I came out here was to save my marriage.'

'Oh?'

'It sounds melodramatic, but it's true. Look, this is rather awkward to talk about, but since you're involved . . .'

'*I'm* involved?' asked Carole.

'No, you're not involved . . . at least, I don't think you are, but you're involved, Jude.'

Jude looked puzzled and felt a little worried. She wasn't sure where this was going.

'Listen,' Henry went on, 'this may be news to you, Carole, but I've known for a long time that Barney and Jude once had an affair.'

'No, it's not news to me,' said Carole pointedly. 'Though I only heard about it last night.'

Jude avoided her friend's eye, focusing on Henry as she said, 'It was a very long time ago. I'm not going to say we didn't have fun at the time, but it's really nothing you should be worrying about.'

'No, I wasn't worried about it when Barney and I first got together. You know, at that stage of a relationship – or certainly once we'd got married – you do all that going through your past emotional entanglements, and everything's fine. Water under the bridge. You feel confident that the relationship you're in now is the one that's going to work, so you can forget about all the baggage from the past. Anyway, the sex was so good, we could even laugh about our previous lovers.'

Some women might have been offended by that, but Jude wasn't. She found it comforting, proof that Barney had no longer been thinking of any ongoing relationship with her.

Henry went on, 'Barney was quite funny about the things he and Nita used to get up to. And I realized that with her it was just sex, there was no real emotional engagement. And they had sex in some fairly bizarre places. Sometimes they'd even link up when she was guiding tour groups to some of the archaeological sites. She'd abandon her punters in an amphitheatre or something while she and Barney nipped off for a quickie.'

Carole and Jude exchanged looks. That fitted in with the scenario for the day of Nita's death.

'I didn't mind hearing about stuff like that,' Henry went on. 'It was funny. And the fact that he made no secret of it, the fact that he didn't hide it from me, that seemed to strengthen our relationship. I just felt so secure with him.

'And that's how it was with Barney and me. It really worked. Different backgrounds and all that, but that seemed to increase the attraction rather than diminish it. We were fine—' she lowered her voice – 'until quite recently.'

'So what happened?' asked Carole flatly.

'Well, the fact is . . .' Henry was once again having difficulty getting the words out. 'The fact is . . . that sex has always been very important to Barney . . .'

Jude didn't think it was the moment to say anything; the subject could all too easily move to the top of a Number twenty-seven bus.

'Very important to me too, as it happens; very important to our relationship. And, anyway, just in the last few months . . . well, not to put too fine a point on it . . . Barney's lost it.'

'Lost what?' asked Carole.

But Jude felt pretty sure that she knew the answer, so she asked bluntly, 'You mean Barney can't get it up any more?'

'Yes. Exactly that. And I don't know what the reason is. Maybe he's under stress with the business, but then he's always been under stress with the business and actually seemed to thrive on it. Or perhaps it's the booze. He's always drunk a lot, though. Mind you, with worrying about his performance in bed, he's drinking even more, which I'm sure doesn't help the situation.'

'No, it wouldn't.'

'And it's having a terrible effect on our marriage. Because he's, like, blaming me for it. I'm not sufficiently stimulating for him in bed. And it's putting terrible stress on me.'

'Was that why you came to see me for the healing?'

Henry Willingdon nodded.

'I thought, with those symptoms, there must be something else you weren't telling me.'

'Well, now you know what it was.'

'And look,' said Jude diffidently, 'now we're on to the subject, you say Barney blames you for what's happening – or not happening?'

'Yes.'

'And has his frustration taken any physical form?'

'What do you mean?'

'Has Barney hit you?'

Henry couldn't put her answer into words, but she nodded slowly, and tears glinted in her eyes.

The same image was going through both Carole and Jude's eyes. In a Lycian tomb at Pinara . . . Barney trying to recapture the wonderful sex he used to have with Nita . . . finding himself unable to deliver . . . blaming her . . . lashing out at her . . . grabbing hold of the lanyard round her neck . . . and twisting and pulling it.

'A little while back you told us,' said Carole, 'that you'd come out here to save your marriage.'

'Yes.'

'I don't see exactly how you were proposing to do that.'

'Well, the worse the . . . all right, I'll use the word – impotence – got, the more Barney blamed me, and the more he also talked about earlier relationships where everything had worked perfectly.'

'Like the one he had with Nita?' Jude suggested.

'Yes. And the one he had with you.'

The scrutiny from Henry's blue eyes was so intense that Jude had to look away.

'Look, I know Barney suggested that you might pick up again, have sex again.'

She couldn't deny it. 'Yes, he did. But I can assure you I made it perfectly clear that there was nothing doing.'

'Barney can be very persistent.'

'I know he can. So can I, though. And when I say "nothing doing", it means "nothing doing".'

Henry Willingdon did seem partially reassured by that. And with relief came a few tears. 'I'm sorry, I just do love Barney so much. And I'm sure I can make our marriage work again.'

'I would think so,' said Carole sniffily. 'Virtually every other advertisement you see in the paper promises to cure "erectile dysfunction".'

'Yes.' Jude's manner was more soothing. 'There's a lot of help to be got out there.'

'I know, but Barney's got that terrible masculine pride. He'd hate going to a doctor and admitting there was anything wrong . . . in that department.'

'I'm sure you could persuade him, Henry.'

'Maybe.' And she did look a little more hopeful.

'In the meantime,' said Carole, 'do you know where Barney is?'

'No. I assume he's staying at Tulip Cottage. But you must

realize I haven't been trying to find him. I don't want him to know I'm here.'

'Well, we went to Tulip Cottage and it was all locked up.'

'Ah. It is quite easy to get in there if you want to try again.'

'Oh?'

'Yes, we always leave a key in the amphora to the right of the front gates.'

'We might try that,' said Carole. 'We certainly do get the impression that Barney's lying low. Jude's tried phoning him a few times, and he hasn't answered.'

'Good.'

'What do you mean?'

'I don't want Barney talking to Jude . . . for reasons which I've just explained.'

'Fine.' Jude paused. 'You know we talked to Fergus yesterday.'

'Yes.'

'And to Kemal. You know who Kemal is?'

'I know who he is. I've never met him.'

'Well, both of them were talking about what happened to Barney's first wife.'

'The rather insignificant Zoë.'

'I don't know whether she was insignificant or not.'

'You'd have to think so if you heard what Barney said about her.'

'Kemal seemed convinced that the accident that happened to her was . . . "arranged".'

'I don't think there's any doubt about that.'

Carole thought it was time for the straight question. 'And was it Barney who "arranged" it?'

Henry looked genuinely shocked. 'Of course not. He didn't go out to Sariyerler that day. He wasn't even in the boat.'

'Then who did arrange it?'

'Nita, obviously. She was Zoë's diving buddy that day. She had the opportunity. She unclasped the weight belt.'

'But why would she do that?'

'Oh, for heaven's sake! Because she loved Barney. She could see things weren't going well between Barney and Zoë. She wanted him all to herself.'

'If she'd do that to one of his wives,' said Carole quietly, 'aren't you worried she might do the same to another one?'

'Yes, I was very worried about that,' Henry Willingdon replied almost smugly. 'But not any more. I know I'm no longer under any threat from Nita Davies.'

TWENTY-FOUR

They couldn't get any more out of Henry about what she meant by that last remark, except that she claimed to have heard Nita was back in England, looking after her sick mother. But she would not say where she'd got that information from.

In fact, she behaved as if her agenda for their meeting had been dealt with and they didn't need to talk any further. Jude reckoned the only item on that agenda had been double-checking whether there was a threat of her ever hooking up again with Barney. Henry seemed to consider that that question had been answered and she felt that her marriage was safe from Jude.

And she seemed equally sure that it was safe from Nita. Carole and Jude discussed that over lunch. Following one of the late tour guide's recommendations, they ate in the Fethiye fish market. Which was excellent.

But they did have a bit of trouble finding it. As they walked through the hot streets of Fethiye, Jude suddenly pointed upwards and burst out laughing.

'What's so funny?'

Jude read the words on the sign. '"TLOS PROPERTY" – isn't that wonderful?'

'In what way?'

'Well, look – "TLOS".'

'Yes, Tlos is a Lycian archaeological site with a Roman Amphitheatre quite near to the seaside resort of Kalkan.'

'No, but don't you see why it's funny . . . with the word "PROPERTY"?'

'It means it's an estate agent, presumably catering for English buyers.'

'I *know* it's an estate agent, but don't you think it looks like a misprint for "LOST PROPERTY"?'

'No,' said Carole.

When they did find it, the Fethiye fish market proved to be a circular tiled building, the central hub of which was a wide circle of fishmongers, surrounded by an outer ring of restaurants against the walls.

Carole was a little inhibited about doing something as ethnic as selecting her own fish, but Jude quickly got into flirtatious banter with one of the salesmen. On his recommendation they each chose a sea bass which looked far too big for a single meal and paid for it from the purple kitty purse.

Then, resisting the blandishments of the other restaurateurs, Carole (who'd consulted her guidebook) walked into one called Reiss Balikcilik. There, Jude ordered another beer ('I really must limit my beer intake soon – but it's just so refreshing') and Carole a glass of white wine ('that one that tastes a bit like Sauvignon Blanc'). *Mezes* and salads arrived as they waited for their fish to be cooked.

'That business about Barney trying to recapture his potency by going back to earlier lovers,' said Carole. 'Did that ring true to you?'

'Oh, yes, I'm afraid so. It would have been in character. And certainly in character for him not to seek medical help for his impotence problem. He'd very much think that was something he could work out for himself – and that it was his wife who was at fault rather than him. A classic case of a bad workman blaming his tools.' Jude giggled. 'Though that's probably not the most apposite expression in the circumstances.'

Their fish arrived. It did look beautifully cooked, and removing the delicious flakes from the bone put a stop to their conversation for a while. Only when the last white morsel had been consumed and their oily lips been wiped clean did Carole say, 'Well, I think our first priority is still to track down Barney.'

'I agree. I'll have one more go at his mobile.'

Jude did. But once again received the message that Barney's phone was switched off.

'So it's back to Tulip Cottage,' said Carole.

'Yes. And let's see if we can find the key in the amphora.'

They could. Both were struck by, but neither commented on, the inconsistency in the Willingdons' attitude to security. The gates and walls of Tulip Cottage protected it as though it were Fort Knox, and yet a key was left readily available in probably the most obvious place for a would-be intruder to look.

They let themselves in and were suitably impressed by the villa that was revealed. Unlike Morning Glory, Tulip Cottage was a completely new build, not based on any existing structures. But it showed the same high spec and meticulous attention to detail. Barney Willingdon's villas were very definitely at the luxury end of the market.

But Carole and Jude didn't have time to take in the beauties of Tulip Cottage. There was something of much more interest on the villa's gravel driveway.

It was Barney's white Range Rover. The driver's side door was open, and there was a neat bullet hole on that side of the windscreen.

As Carole and Jude drew closer, they saw that all the 4 x 4's tyres were flat, as if they too had been shot at.

On the headrest and back of the driver's seat were still-wet traces of blood.

Of Barney himself there was no sign.

The women were too shocked to speak, but both turned at the sound of a house door opening.

Erkan had just come out on to the terrace. In his hand there was a pistol.

TWENTY-FIVE

'What are you doing here?' he asked in surprisingly good English. He reached up with his free hand to touch a cut on his forehead. The hand came away with blood on it. He swayed slightly.

'Perhaps you'd better sit down.' Jude came towards him. He waved her away with the gun, but staggered a bit and did go and sit on one of the poolside chairs.

'We came here looking for Barney,' said Carole.

'So did I.' His voice was a bit blurred, dozy from the blow he'd received.

Jude gestured to the car. 'It looks as if you found him.'

'Yes, I found him. And I shot at him. But he escaped.'

'Well, look,' said Carole in her most reasonable voice. 'If it was Barney you wanted to shoot, then presumably you don't want to shoot us.'

'No,' Erkan conceded.

'Then perhaps you would be so good as to put that gun down.'

He couldn't see a reason why he shouldn't accede to her request, so he laid the pistol on the small table at his side. 'I will find him, though,' he asserted, 'and kill him.'

'Are you sure you haven't already killed him?' asked Carole. 'There is blood on the seat of his car.'

'No. When he see me, he gets into car to drive away. I shoot tyres to stop him. Then I shoot at him through windscreen, but he is getting out of car and I only hit his shoulder, I think. Then he throws stone at me.' He gestured up to his bleeding forehead. 'For a moment I pass out. When I come round, no sign of Barney. I go in house, look for him, he not there.'

'May I ask,' asked Jude gently, 'why you want to kill him?'

'He kill my wife,' came the simple reply.

'Are you sure he did? Did you see him kill her?'

'No, but I know when they were to meet – eleven o'clock.

And I know where – the tomb. And that is where I find Nita's body. He must have killed her.'

'You are talking,' asked Carole, 'about the Lycian tomb at Pinara.'

'Yes. How do you know this?'

'Because I went there. I found your wife's body.'

Erkan looked puzzled and even more confused. 'How you know she would be there?'

'I didn't know. Well, actually, I had heard she was taking a tour group to Pinara that day, but I was just looking at the tomb because it's one of the few there that's accessible.'

'I do not understand. When you see Nita, she is dead?'

'Yes. Strangled by the lanyard of her ID card.'

'That is how she was killed, yes. But you don't see Barney?'

'No. What's more, I didn't see his Range Rover in the car park.'

'There are other places to park, many ways to get into the Pinara site.'

'When Jude and I got back to the tomb that afternoon, it was empty. No sign that Nita had ever been there. Did you bring her body back?'

'No.'

'Then who did?'

'Barney, I suppose. He is murderer, needs to hide body.'

'And where do you think he might have hidden it?'

Erkan shrugged. 'There are many old quarries and cliffs and bays. Here is not a difficult place to hide a body. I will find Nita's body. More important, though, first I will find Barney and kill him.'

'Don't you think,' suggested Carole, 'it might make more sense to call in the police?'

'No. No need for police. This is personal matter. Barney shame me by having affair with my wife. She tell me is all over. Then I discover she has set up to meet him again. That is why I must kill him. No one treat a Turkish man like he treat me and get away with it.'

'So first you wanted to kill him for having an affair with your wife. Then you want to kill him for killing your wife.'

'Yes.'

'But you must see the two cases are different. Adultery is morally wrong, a sin, perhaps, but murder is definitely a crime. Why not get your revenge on Barney by going to the police and—?'

'No, it is personal revenge. I will kill him!'

'You'll have to find him first,' said Jude.

'I will find him. He walked away from here. He is on foot; he has not got a car. Someone in Kayaköy will have seen him.'

'But if you do kill him, you'll go to prison for a long time.'

'I do not care. I will have had my revenge.'

'One thing I don't understand . . .' said Carole. 'After you had found your wife's body, did you go looking for Barney at Pinara?'

'I look a little. But then I reckon he has come back to Kayaköy. I come back to look for him here.'

'Just leaving Nita's body in the tomb?'

'Yes. I am angry. I am furious. I am not thinking straight.'

'So you have no proof that Barney removed the body?'

'I don't need proof. It must be him. Who else knows the body is there?'

Which, Carole and Jude reflected, was a very good question.

Erkan stood up. 'Now I will go and find him.' But the sudden movement was too much. He swayed and stumbled to the ground.

Jude was quickly by his side. 'It's your head wound. You must get it seen to.'

'No, I have to . . .' But the sentence was mumbled away.

'We must call you an ambulance.'

'No, I can't . . .' His words were slurring now.

'Tell us what number we call for an ambulance,' said Carole.

Erkan didn't resist any more, but just managed to get out the numbers.

Carole rang through. To her surprise, the call was answered by someone who spoke good English. She was told that the ambulance would be there within half an hour.

Then Erkan passed out. They took the gun and, unable to think of anywhere else, they put it in the glove compartment of their car.

When the ambulance arrived, neither the driver nor his fellow paramedic spoke English, so Carole and Jude were not required to provide any explanations about why they were at Tulip Cottage. The assumption was presumably made that they were renting it.

Erkan stirred a little when he was stretchered to the ambulance. Jude did not think his injury was life-threatening, probably just a case of concussion. But he certainly did need professional attention.

The women gave their mobile numbers to the ambulance men and mimed that they would like to be kept informed of the patient's progress. Whether they were understood or not, they didn't know.

TWENTY-SIX

They didn't know what to do, but they knew they had to do something. Whatever crimes Barney Willingdon might have committed, he certainly did not deserve to die. And, though Carole's attitude was not so forgiving, Jude still retained a strong affection for him. Somehow they had to save him from a scuba diving instructor with a gun. Because, although Erkan was currently hors de combat, they both knew that they had not heard the last of him. He still wanted to have his revenge.

The minute they were back in the car, Jude tried ringing Barney on his mobile, but she had exactly the same response as before. Wherever he was, he wasn't taking calls.

As they turned off the main road up towards Morning Glory, Carole said, 'I feel so isolated. We have no network here. We don't know anyone. If we did want to contact the police, I really wouldn't know how to set about it.'

'Well, we do have one contact . . .'

'Who?'

'Our friendly – perhaps over-friendly – expatriate neighbour.'

Carole shuddered. 'Travers Hughes-Swann.'

'He does speak English. And he seems to know everything that goes on in Kayaköy. It's worth asking.'

So rather than continuing to Morning Glory, the car turned off towards Brighton House. The main building looked more like a cowshed than ever, and the owner's stone garden features didn't look any better than they had on the women's previous visit.

Travers himself was tending a barbecue which he appeared to have just lit. He'd apparently taken a break in his gardening because there were piles of culled weeds on the footpath. He was wearing his uniform of shorts, socks and sandals, and his head looked more like a pickled walnut than ever.

But he was very pleased at what he saw arriving. 'Two lovely ladies. To what do I owe my good fortune?'

'We just wondered if you could help us out?' said Jude. 'You know, with your local knowledge?'

'Always happy to oblige, particularly when the request comes from personages of such pulchritude.' He indicated the barbecue. 'Just preparing supper for myself and "Her Indoors".'

'Well, if we're delaying you, please don't—'

'No, no. Barbecue takes a while to heat up. I'm in no hurry.' He gestured to the chairs in his 'suntrap' (though at that time of day his travesty of a Lycian tomb was in the shade) and all three of them sat down.

'Could I offer you a cup of tea or—?'

Remembering the chipped cups of their previous visit, both women politely demurred.

'So what can I do you for?' he said with a kind of pub bore's heartiness.

'Well, look, it's all rather complicated,' Carole began. 'It's about Barney.'

'Surprise, surprise.'

'Why do you say that?'

Travers shrugged. 'It's not like you two have a lot of other contacts out here, is it? And Barney's a kind of larger-than-life figure who attracts attention wherever he goes.'

'Yes,' Jude agreed. 'Which makes it rather strange that we haven't been able to contact him for the last couple of days.'

'He's got business interests in other parts of Turkey. He may be away from Kayaköy for a few days.'

'But he isn't answering his mobile.'

'Ah. Well, yes, that might be rather out of character. So what do you think might have happened to him?'

Carole and Jude exchanged covert looks, both trying to work out how much they should tell Travers. 'The fact is, we do know where he's just been,' Carole began cautiously.

'That sounds intriguing.' He rubbed his leathery hands together. 'And mysterious.'

'We went down to Tulip Cottage to see if he was there. We tried the call button on the entryphone,' she went on, slightly editing the truth, 'and got no reply, but Barney had told us there was a key.'

'In the amphora to the right of the gates,' said Travers, once again proving that there were no secrets in Kayaköy.

'Yes. So we went in. And we didn't find Barney there, but we did find Erkan. You know who we mean by—?'

'Of course. Runs the diving school. Nita's husband.'

'Well, he had a gun with him, and he said he was going to kill Barney.'

'Oh.' Travers looked more alert as he asked, 'Did he say why?'

'He accused Barney of having killed his wife.'

'Did he? And do you have any idea why Erkan believes that Nita is dead?'

Some instinct for caution stopped Carole from admitting what she had seen in the tomb at Pinara. Instead, she lied, 'I've no idea what made him think that she is.'

'Hm.' Travers Hughes-Swann looked thoughtful. 'And you say you've come here to benefit from my local knowledge. What do you actually want me to do?'

'Find Barney. We thought you might know where he would go if he was on the run from Erkan.'

He patted his chin complacently. 'I might have some thoughts on that, yes.'

'And, more generally,' said Jude, 'tell us what we ought to do. Should we be getting in touch with the police?'

He looked surprised. 'Why would you want to do that?'

'Well, if there's a homicidal Erkan with a gun out to kill Barney, don't you think the police should be notified to avert a disaster?'

Travers Hughes-Swann shook his head slowly. 'I wouldn't necessarily say that that was how things are done out here.'

'Oh?' said Carole, once again thinking of *Midnight Express*, the film she had never seen. Visions of corrupt and brutal policemen filled her mind.

'Don't worry,' said Travers. 'I'll make a few phone calls, check things out. I'm sure I can find where Barney is.'

'Well, I hope you can,' said Jude. 'And before Erkan does.'

'I'll do my best. Wouldn't want to let down two ladies as lovely as you are, would I?'

Both Carole and Jude tried to smile, with limited success.

He looked across to the barbecue, from which there was now less smoke as the charcoal burned through. 'As I said, I was just about to cook something for myself and Phyllis. You'd be most welcome to join me for a light supper if—'

Visions of the chipped cups they had been given on their last visit prompted quick responses from both of them. It was very kind, but they'd had a late lunch.

Travers Hughes-Swann saw them the short distance to their car, again asking, 'And, apart from what Erkan said, you have no other reason to believe that his wife Nita is dead?'

They denied hotly that they had. But they still thought it was a slightly odd question to ask.

Back at Morning Glory both the women were restless. They had done what they could in their search for Barney, but it didn't seem to be much. And their distaste for Travers Hughes-Swann made them feel slightly uncomfortable about having involved him in their investigation. They couldn't be certain about his allegiances. Maybe he might support Erkan against Barney.

They both had a swim to wash off the day's stickiness. Then, while Carole took a shower, Jude lay in her bikini on a lounger, soaking in the day's last rays of sun. It was while she was lying there that her mobile rang.

'Hello?'

'Jude, it's me, Barney.' His voice was a whisper, tight with emotion.

'God. Where on earth are you?'

'I'm in a safe place. At least, safe for the moment. But I need you to help me. I've had an accident and cut myself. Trouble is, I'm losing a lot of blood.'

'I know what's happened to you. It wasn't an accident. You've been shot by Erkan.'

'How the hell do you know that?'

'Doesn't matter. Where are you?'

'As I say, I'm in a safe place. But I'll be moving again shortly. Can you bring some bandages or plasters or something, just to stop this bleeding? You'll find them in the kitchen drawer at Morning Glory – though, of course, I don't know if you are at Morning Glory.'

'Yes, I am. And presumably you're not far away? Since you didn't have a car with you when you left Tulip Cottage.'

'How do you know all this about where I've been?'

'We met Erkan.'

'Oh my God!' There was naked terror in the voice. 'He's not there with you, is he?'

'No.'

'That's a relief.'

'Perhaps not quite such a great relief. He'll soon be out there looking for you again.'

'He won't find me. Or, at least, he won't find me when I've made my next move.'

'Look, can't someone just talk to him? Stop this absurd game of Cops and Robbers?'

'No. He's dangerous.'

'He's also convinced that you murdered Nita.'

But Barney didn't have any response to that. He just said, 'Get here as soon as possible, Jude.'

'Fine for you to say that, but I don't know where "here" is, do I?'

'Get down to the Antik restaurant . . . You know where I mean?'

'Yes.'

'Either you'll get another call from me, or someone'll point you in the right direction.'

'Who?'

'Most important of all, don't tell anyone you've heard from me. And come on your own.'

'But I can't—'

'I've got to go.' And the line went dead.

Jude sat there for a moment in shock. She tried to call him back, but got no response.

The box of medical equipment was where he'd said it would be. As she went upstairs to change, Jude tried to think of what she could say to Carole. There was no way 'just nipping out for a walk' would avoid follow-up questions. She'd have to come up with something better than that.

But when, once dressed, she crossed the landing towards Carole's room, she saw that the problem had been solved for her. Wrapped only in a bath towel, her friend lay on the bed fast asleep. She must have had her shower and just laid down on the bed for a couple of minutes, and the shocks and stresses of the previous days had caught up with her.

Blessing her good fortune, Jude tiptoed back downstairs and set out in the moonlit evening to walk through Kayaköy.

TWENTY-SEVEN

Carole woke some half an hour later and at first she could not think where she was. The moon was bright enough to shed rectangles of light across the bed, and the net curtains stirred in the warm evening breeze. She felt down her body, and the touch of towel told her she was in her bedroom at Morning Glory.

With the realization came an instinctive guilt. She shouldn't be lying around sleeping in the daytime! (Carole Seddon had never really caught on to the concept of holidays.) So she quickly got up and dressed.

It was clear when she got downstairs that Jude was not about. And, with even more guilt, Carole recognized that her first reaction was one of relief. Much as she liked – possibly even loved, though she didn't go in for that sentimental stuff – her friend, she wasn't used to being in anyone's company twenty-four hours a day. And just as she had felt the need to go to Pinara alone on the Tuesday morning, so she once again felt grateful for a little solitude.

Then she felt a knee-jerk twinge of anxiety. Jude hadn't gone off with Barney, had she? But she was quickly reassured. Barney was a man on the run; no need to worry about him and Jude becoming emotionally entangled again.

Feeling daringly self-indulgent, Carole went to the fridge and poured herself a large glass of the wine that tasted like Sauvignon Blanc. She took a sip as she moved to sit outside. It really did taste astoundingly good. Could it be that her long-term loyalty to Chilean Chardonnay was being challenged?

She sat in an upright chair by the pool and made a conscious effort to relax. Then she remembered that she should have sprayed on some mosquito repellent. But she resisted the impulse to go upstairs and get it.

Perhaps she ought to be doing a *Times* crossword . . .? Again she suppressed the urge to move. Because in order to see enough to enable her to do the *Times* crossword, she would have to put on the outside lights, and the outside lights would attract mosquitoes which would mean she'd also have to spray herself with mosquito repellent.

No, better just to sit there. She tried to let the tension drain out of her body, but her body was stiffened by many years of keeping it all in. She felt sure Jude would know some mumbo-jumbo like tantric breathing to relax her body, but then Carole Seddon wasn't Jude and, she assured herself, never wanted to be.

She took a long swallow from her wine glass. Followed it by another. Yes, that helped. For a moment she really did feel quite relaxed.

Then she smelt burning.

TWENTY-EIGHT

I t was a beautiful moonlit walk through Kayaköy from Morning Glory to the foot of the ghost town. There were even fireflies to be seen amidst the trees. But Jude was unaware of any of it. Her mind was too full.

Increasingly, it looked as though Barney Willingdon had been responsible for the murder of Nita Davies. Erkan's logic had been convincing, and Henry's suggested scenario of Barney turning on his mistress in frustration at his inability to function sexually did have a horrible ring of truth about it.

But there remained elements that were unexplained. And she still had difficulty in casting Barney, a man she had once loved, in the role of murderer.

Nor did it ever occur to her that going to meet him in this clandestine way might be putting her own life at risk.

Her mobile phone stayed obstinately silent. As she approached the flat area beneath the ghost town where the camels had hunkered down for the night, she tried ringing Barney's number. But there was still no reply.

He'd said either he'd contact her or someone would 'point her in the right direction'. In other words, she could do nothing by her own efforts, just sit and wait.

At least she could do that with a drink in her hand. There were a few more people in Antik that evening. By the fire, two women were busy pouring batter for *gözleme*. Jude decided she would order a white wine, but the owner, seeing her arrive, was already pouring her a cold Efes, so she didn't argue when he brought it to the table.

'Your friend is joining you?'

'No, just me tonight. And just for a drink.'

'Fine,' he said and moved across to a table of German tourists who were noisily calling for more drinks.

Another man moved so silently that she was hardly aware of him until he was sitting on the chair next to her.

'Hello,' he whispered. 'I have found Barney.'

It was Travers Hughes-Swann.

Jude swallowed down half of her beer and left some lira on the table to pay for it. Then she and Travers slipped away into the darkness. They passed by the battered Land Rover, which must have already been parked there when Jude arrived. Uncomfortably aware of the odour emanating from Travers' body, she followed him to the edge of the flat area where the path led up into the ghost town.

'He's up in there, is he?'

Travers put a finger to his lips and nodded.

The soft soles of their shoes made no sound on the well-worn cobbles of the street. The moonlight was strong enough to show any unevenness in the path ahead. The noise from the restaurants below was filtered and thin, as if coming from a distant island. They passed the gaping windows of the roofless houses and, though Jude didn't much care for Travers, she was grateful not to be alone in this necromantic landscape.

They climbed higher than she and Carole had done a few nights before. They went past the tall Greek Orthodox church and climbed on.

A sudden movement and clattering in the pathside grasses set Jude's nerves jangling.

'Just a goat,' murmured Travers.

Then the road ahead of them was closed. Only by red and white tape on metal poles, but the hazard symbols and notices in English declared the area to be unsafe.

'Is he up there?' whispered Jude.

'Yes. Do you want me to come with you?'

'No. I think it'd be better if I talked to him on my own.'

'Are you sure? Are you sure he's not dangerous?'

'No. I don't think I'm in any danger. I really cannot believe that Barney murdered Nita.'

'Oh? Do you know who did then?'

'No. I just can't work it out. Who killed her, and who moved the body.'

'What makes you think the body was moved?'

Jude gave him a brief summary of Carole's initial discovery and their fruitless trip back to Pinara on the Tuesday afternoon.

'Hm. That's interesting.' But not interesting enough for him to ask any further questions. Travers Hughes-Swann pointed ahead, beyond the tape, where the uneven track climbed higher. 'Go up there. Just round the corner on the left there's a house whose door frame is still intact. Barney's in there.'

'OK.'

'I'll stay here on guard.'

'Thank you. And thank you very much for finding him.'

'The pleasure's all mine. Particularly when I am doing it for such a lovely lady,' he added, losing most of the brownie points he'd been accumulating of the previous half-hour.

Jude nodded thanks to him, bent down to get under the red and white tape and started on up the hill.

TWENTY-NINE

Carole had a pretty good idea of where the smell of burning was coming from. And, sure enough, when she entered the gates of Brighton House, there was a small bonfire blazing in front of the building.

It didn't look as if it was about to burn the place down. Carole found a bucket, filled it with water in the kitchen and soon put out the blaze. The charcoal on the barbecue was still hot and red. She reckoned an ember must have spat out or fallen on to the dry garden rubbish nearby. No big disaster, just a strong whiff of burning.

She was turning back towards Morning Glory when she suddenly had a thought. Of course, Travers's bedridden wife Phyllis must be in the house. How terrifying might it be for someone unable to move to smell smoke from downstairs?

Carole didn't know the extent of the woman's disabilities. The fact that she had heard no shouts for help or screams might mean that she was unable to speak. That would make the smell of smoke and the flicker of the flames even more horrible.

Carole knew it was her duty to see that Phyllis Hughes-Swann was all right.

The interior of Brighton House, revealed by the moonlight through the windows, was considerably smaller than that of Morning Glory. It was basically one room with a kitchen area to the back. Apart from the front entrance, the only other door led off to a not very salubrious lavatory.

But then Carole had not really expected to find Phyllis Hughes-Swann on the ground floor. She switched on the light that shone down on the staircase and made her way up.

There were three doors off the landing, all closed. The one ahead proved to be a shower room which smelt of damp. The sweaty smell released by the next door announced to Carole that she was in Travers's bedroom. There was a single metal-framed bed with grubby sheets, an open cupboard and a selection of unsavoury garments, mostly pairs of shorts, scattered across the floor.

Carole moved across the landing to the other room, opened the door and switched on the light.

It was a workshop. Central was a wooden sawing bench. A variety of tools for carpentry and gardening hung from the walls. Paint pots stood on shelves. The floor was littered with sawdust and shavings.

On a tripod near the window stood a fairly sophisticated telescope, trained, Carole noted with a sickening feeling, in the direction of Morning Glory. Other telescopes, binoculars, cameras and a couple of laptops were scattered on a table nearby. There were earphones too, plugged into some kind of receiver.

There was no bed in the room, no sign of human habitation.

Whether or not Phyllis Hughes-Swann had ever lived in Brighton House, she was no longer in residence.

THIRTY

Barney Willingdon had lost a lot of blood. Though Erkan's bullet had only scraped his shoulder it had caused a disproportionate amount of bleeding. Jude patched it up as best she could, wishing she'd thought to bring a torch with her from Morning Glory. Thank God, at least, the moon was nearly full.

She waited until she'd done the repairs before saying, 'Calm down. You're safe from Erkan, at least for the time being.'

Panic flickered in Barney's eyes. He looked pathetic, his long hair flattened by sweat, his beard ragged. 'So where is he now?'

'He's in hospital in Fethiye being patched up after you hit him on the head with a stone.'

That news brought a moment of relief before the paranoia returned. 'But he'll still come after me as soon as he's able to.'

'Yes, I think you're probably right. Let's just hope he's kept in hospital a long time.'

'Hm.' But Barney didn't sound reassured.

'What I can't understand,' said Jude, 'is why you have to hide away like this. I thought everyone out here in Kayaköy was one of your mates. There must be lots who'd take you in, look after you, keep you safe from Erkan.'

'No, it doesn't work like that out here. Yes, they're all my mates while we're in business, while that business is going well, but they've got their own code too, and if you break that they can get nasty. They're all related, you see, all cousins. They weren't worried about me having an affair with Nita. They thought that was funny if anything, putting Erkan in the traditional role of the cuckold. But if he's going round saying I killed his wife, that would be very different. All of my so-called friends will quickly become my enemies. There's nobody I can trust out here now.'

'Except Travers Hughes-Swann?'

'Well, he's just a convenience. He tracked me down here.'

'How did he know this was where you'd be?'

'Oh, for reasons that go back a long way. The details aren't important. I just saw a way of using him to get you up here.'

'And he's not in with the locals? He's not likely to tell Erkan or his relatives where you are?'

'God knows. I bloody hope not.'

'But do you trust him?'

'I have to. As I say, he found me here. So to some extent I'm at his mercy.'

'Hm.' Jude was silent. They heard another clatter of goat's hoofs on rock. 'And you say the reason why Erkan wants to kill you is because he thinks you murdered his wife?'

'Yes.'

'Well, I suppose a question I do have to ask, Barney, is: did you murder Nita?'

'No, I didn't.' But he spoke with despair rather than anger. 'Look, how much do you know about what happened on Tuesday?'

'Quite a bit. Carole and I have been doing a lot of investigating.'

'Why?'

'Because Carole found Nita's body that morning.'

'Good God, how?'

'Pure coincidence. She'd decided, in a very Carole way, that she didn't want to stay around Morning Glory and untwitch – which was all I wanted to do – but she wanted to go and look around Pinara.'

'And she went to the tomb?'

'Yes, she said it was one of the few that were accessible.'

Barney sighed desolately.

'We also know that you and Nita used to use that place for assignations.'

'How the hell did you find that out?'

Jude just said that they'd found Nita's dedicated mobile phone. 'And you were presumably "L"?'

'Yes.'

'Would I regret asking for a reason for that?'

He looked embarrassed. 'It was a kind of pet name. Something to do with "Lycia".'

'I see.' Jude was cautious about bringing Henry into the conversation yet as she continued her explanation. 'So we knew that you'd set up to meet Nita at eleven o'clock on that Tuesday morning – though, of course, Carole had no idea of that when she discovered the body. So did you meet? Did you and Nita have your encounter?'

Barney shook his head miserably. He was so reduced, so far from the cocksure Barney Willingdon Jude had known that she couldn't help feeling a pang of sympathy for him.

'What happened?'

'She was already dead when I got there. Strangled with that lanyard thing that she . . .' He broke into sobs.

'So what did you do?'

'I don't know. I didn't know what to do. I was, like, dazed. I went back to the car – which I'd parked in a place I knew, away from the car park – and, I don't know, I just drove around aimlessly.'

'Did you move her body?'

'No. I knew it was a crime scene. I knew nothing should be touched.'

'But did you report what you had found to the police?'

'No.'

'Why not?'

'I didn't want anyone to know I'd been there. I knew that could make me look like a suspect.'

'And when we asked where she was you fobbed us off with that story about her having gone back to England to nurse her sick mother?'

'Yes, it was all I could think of on the spur of the moment. So then I just waited, thinking that someone else would find her, that the police would be called in, that I'd hear about it on the news or the local grapevine.'

'But you haven't heard anything?'

'No.'

'And why do you think that is?'

He shrugged. 'Maybe her body hasn't been found yet.'

'Not that. It's been moved. It was moved later in the day you found it.'

'Who by?'

'We have no idea. Though you were one of the people we thought was in the frame for having done it.'

'I'm sorry. You're not making sense. What do you mean?'

So Jude explained how Carole had returned from Pinara to Kayaköy and how they'd both gone back to the scene of the crime to find nothing but the mobile phone.

'So, before it was moved, your friend Carole saw the body, I saw the body. Who else?'

'Erkan did.'

'Which is why he's trying to kill me, I know.'

There was a silence in the ghost town. Then Jude said, 'Could we go back a bit, to what happened to your first wife?'

'Yes,' he said wretchedly.

'I've heard about the circumstances. From Kemal.'

'Good God. How the hell did you get on to him?'

'That's not important. But he seemed pretty convinced that Zoë's death was not accidental.'

'That happens every time there's a scuba diving accident. The conspiracy theorists go mad.'

'But what Kemal said was quite convincing. Those weight belts don't drop off of their own accord.'

'No,' he agreed sullenly.

'So it's another of those questions I have to ask you, Barney. Did you arrange Zoë's death?'

'No, I bloody didn't!' He sounded genuinely outraged by the suggestion. 'Things hadn't been going well between us, we'd talked about divorce, but I'd never do that.'

'So did Nita do it off her own bat?'

He was silent, then said, 'It could have been a genuine accident.'

'Yes?'

'Yes.' But he wasn't even convincing himself. 'I try not to think about it, but yes, I'm afraid Nita probably did.'

'And have you ever been afraid that Nita might have been planning some similar fate for Henry?'

'No.'

'She was very possessive. About you. Even when you'd married her off to Erkan and bought them the diving school, it was still you she hoped to end up with.'

'I don't know about that. Anyway, what's all of this got to do with Nita's murder?'

'I spoke to Henry about it.'

'Henry? My wife Henry? When?'

Jude was amazed to find herself replying, 'This morning.' So much seemed to have happened since then.

'What? You phoned Chantry House?'

'No. Henry's out here.'

'Is she?' Once again he sounded genuinely shocked.

'She's staying at the Hotel Osman in Fethiye. And she's got Fergus McNally with her.'

'What? Look, if you're trying to persuade me that my wife would have an affair with a loser like—'

'That is not what I'm saying. There's no affair. It's a business relationship. Henry paid for Fergus's flights, and she's also paying him to do some work for her.'

'What kind of work?'

'That's what I've been wondering. Some kind of investigative work. Part of it was finding out what happened on that day at Sariyerler when Zoë died.'

'And the other part?'

'I don't know for sure, but I do know Henry had been very concerned about the possibility of Nita trying to eliminate her as well. Had been, I say, but this morning she announced with great satisfaction that she was no longer worried about any threat from Nita.'

'So are you suggesting that my wife Henry actually paid Fergus to . . .?'

'Well, it's a possibility,' said Jude.

THIRTY-ONE

Carole, in a state of some confusion, was just leaving the front door of Brighton House when she saw the outline of its owner coming through the main gates.

'Good evening,' he said. 'Funny, I hadn't got you down as the burglarious sort.'

'No, I'm not. I came in because I smelt burning and . . .' She indicated the pile of dampened-down ash. 'I think a bit of charcoal must have fallen out of the barbecue and set it alight. I was afraid the house might have caught fire, so I came to put it out.'

'Well, that was very public-spirited of you. Thank you very much. What a good person you are to have as a neighbour – and not only because of your pulchritude.'

Carole suppressed a shudder. 'Well, I'd better get back to Morning Glory. Jude went out for a walk, I think, but she's probably back now and I—'

'No, she's not back yet. I've just taken her to see Barney Willingdon.'

Carole was too tense to worry that Jude was progressing on their investigation in a major way without her. 'Really?' she said. 'How on earth did you know where he was?'

'Oh, I make it my business to know about everything that goes on in Kayaköy.'

'Good. Well, I'd better get back and . . .'

But Travers Hughes-Swann was still standing in her way, firmly in the middle of the two open gates. 'While, as I say, I'm very grateful to your public spirit in coming to put out the fire, I do find myself faced by a small niggling question.'

'And what's that?' asked Carole, trying to sound casual.

'It's simply: in what way did your coming to put out the fire necessitate your entering my house?'

There was no way of avoiding the direct question. 'To be quite honest, I was worried about your wife.'

'Ah. "Her Indoors",' he said.

'Yes.'

'Or should it be "Her Not Indoors"?'

Her second, 'Yes,' was almost inaudible.

'I think we need to talk about this, Carole,' said Travers Hughes-Swann.

The discussion of murder in the ghost town seemed to have transmuted into a kind of therapy session. Jude told Barney the content of their conversation with Henry that morning, and he admitted his terrible fear of impotence. And, yes, he had tried to pick up again with Nita – because he wanted to recapture the past, to go back to the days when sex had been instinctive and natural.

'I think you need to talk to Henry,' said Jude.

'I have talked to her till I'm blue in the face. It doesn't make any difference.'

'Talk to her about the problem. The sex problem. You need professional help.'

'What, you mean I need to go to some smug eleven-year-old doctor,' he asked scornfully, 'and tell her I can't get it up?'

'It needn't be like that.' Instinctively, Jude had started talking in her healer's voice. 'There are medical specialists in that kind of area.'

He snorted contempt.

'Anyway, apart from that, why don't you ring Henry?'

'Why?'

'Well, she's here. She's only in Fethiye. She can rescue you, take you to the Hotel Osman for the rest of the night, and you can get a flight back to England tomorrow.'

'I don't know. If it was Henry who organized Nita's death, then—'

'It was not Henry who organized the death. You killed her!'

They both looked up at the sound, to see a figure framed in the rotting doorway. The bandage round his head looked like a turban in the moonlight. In his hand was a gun.

It was Erkan.

*   *   *

'Your friend gave you away,' said Travers Hughes-Swann.

'I don't know what you mean.'

'The lovely Jude. She told me about you finding the body.'

'I still don't understand.'

'Everyone seems to think that Barney killed Nita. That's the logical thing to think. And once Erkan has killed Barney, the whole affair will be neatly sewn up without any involvement of the police . . . well, except when they arrest Erkan.'

'Erkan's in hospital in Fethiye. He can't do much harm to Barney at the moment.'

'Don't you believe it. I phoned him as soon as your friend Jude told me about you discovering the body. I told him all the details, and I told him that Barney must have killed Nita. As a result, he discharged himself from hospital and got a cousin of his to drive him back to Kayaköy.' Travers looked at his watch. 'Barney is probably already dead.'

'But does anyone know where Barney is? How's Erkan going to find him?'

'I know where Barney is. In the ghost town. I've told Erkan where to find him.'

'Why on earth did you do that?'

'I told you. So that the whole business is neatly sewn up. Erkan kills Barney for strangling Nita. The police arrest Erkan.' He spread his hands wide. 'How tidy is that?'

'It won't be so tidy,' said Carole, 'if I tell the police about finding the body.'

'No, I agree, it won't.'

And suddenly he had grabbed her, enveloping her in his body odour. Carole tried to fight back, but there was amazing strength in his wiry tanned arms. He must have had the plastic garden ties ready, because soon she was pinned down in an upright chair, wrists and ankles strapped to its arms and legs.

'Which is why,' said Travers, as if there had been no interruption to their conversation, 'I have to ensure that you don't go to the police.'

'Are you threatening to murder me?'

He smiled ruefully in the moonlight. 'I'm afraid I can't see any other viable alternative.'

'Suppose I were to promise you that I won't go to the police, that I will forget what I saw at Pinara?'

'Oh, if only one could trust people's promises,' he said almost wistfully.

'So did you actually strangle Nita?' asked Carole.

'Yes,' he replied with something approaching satisfaction.

'But why? Why were you at Pinara, anyway?'

'Ooh, there's a long history of me going to Pinara, you know, Carole.'

'What, as a sightseer?'

This seemed to amuse him. 'No, not as a sightseer . . . more to see the sights.'

'What do you mean?'

'That Lycian tomb where Nita died has seen a lot of action over the years.'

'You mean sexual action between her and Barney?'

'Yes, that's exactly what I mean. How did you find out about that?' Carole clearly didn't think it was the moment for long explanations, so he went on, 'I first came across them by accident. I was there sightseeing, with Phyllis. Just before we got to the car park on our way back, I needed to nip into the woods to have a pee. I saw the little stream, and then through the trees I could see into the tomb.' He chuckled again. 'And see what was going on in the tomb. I didn't have any of my equipment with me then, but I still found what I saw very exciting. So the next time the two of them were there I saw to it that I was properly equipped.'

'But how did you know when they were going to be there?'

'Not too difficult to work out. As I may have said, there are no secrets in Kayaköy, so everyone would know when Barney Willingdon was going to be over here. And the schedules of the tours Nita organized were easy enough to access – from holiday companies' brochures at first, and later on their websites.

'And Barney and Nita were very regular in their assignations. Eleven o'clock in the morning. Nita would send her tour party off to look at the amphitheatre with the junior guide, then she'd go to the tomb to meet Barney. And I'd be ready waiting with my equipment.'

'When you say "equipment",' asked Carole with distaste, 'what do you mean?'

'Binoculars, cameras – particularly cameras.' He sniggered. 'With telephoto lenses, of course.'

'So you mean you've got a whole archive of . . .?'

'Yes,' he said complacently.

It was at that moment Carole realized just how unhinged Travers Hughes-Swann was. And how little hope she had of avoiding the fate he had lined up for her.

'For some years,' he continued, 'there wasn't any activity at the tomb. If Barney came over with his wife – the first one or the second one – he wouldn't make his assignations at Pinara. But this time I knew he'd come over on his own, and then I heard Nita say that she was going to Pinara on Tuesday.'

Fairly sure she wouldn't like the answer, Carole asked, 'When you said you "heard Nita", where were you when you heard her?'

'Right here,' he said smugly. 'I have microphones set up in Morning Glory. I like to know what's going on.'

Carole felt physically sick at the thought that this pervert could have been listening to every word she and Jude uttered when they were at the villa. She was grateful that none of their poolside conjectures had featured him as a possible murderer. Otherwise the schedule for her execution might have been moved forward a bit.

Still, she might as well go to her death knowing the solution to the murder mystery she'd become involved in, so she asked bluntly, 'Why did you kill Nita?'

'Ah.' He sounded almost apologetic as he said, 'Bit of a cock-up on my efficiency front, I'm afraid. There's an optimum position in the woods near that Lycian tomb, just over the little stream, where I always set up my equipment, but some trees had fallen down there, so it wasn't terribly safe underfoot. And I'm afraid, just after Nita had got to the tomb, I slipped, and she heard the noise and came out. Then she saw me. And once she'd seen me . . .' He spread his hands wide in a gesture of inevitability. 'Well, there was only one thing I could do, wasn't there?'

Carole could think of a wide choice of things that could

have been done by someone less insane than Travers Hughes-Swann, but she didn't enumerate them. Instead, boldly, she asked, 'And did you kill your wife Phyllis too?'

'Oh, you're very quick, Carole. Yes, I'm afraid again I had to.'

'Why?'

'Well, she found my archive.'

'I beg your pardon?'

'She was looking at my laptop – which I'd many times told her she shouldn't do – and she came across the archive of photographs.'

'The ones you'd shot at Pinara?'

'Amongst others. Amongst many others. You'd be surprised how many people leave their bedroom windows open at night when they're in a hot country like Turkey. And I have very good telephoto lenses on my cameras and video cameras.' He giggled at his own cleverness.

'And did you strangle your wife too?'

'Yes,' he replied. 'It's the easiest way.' Then, to Carole's horror, he reached into the pocket of his grubby shorts and produced something she recognized. It was the lanyard from which Nita Davies's ID card used to hang.

'And you maintained that your wife was still alive so that there'd be no enquiry into her death?'

'Well, that was part of the reason,' he admitted. 'But also the state pension is rather more generous for a married couple than it is for a single person.' He spoke as if all of his behaviour had been prompted by pure mathematical logic.

'And it was you, Travers, who removed Nita's body from the tomb?'

'Yes. Well, I had to, didn't I? Can't leave dead bodies in Lycian tombs, can you?' He seemed to find this very funny. 'I brought her back in the Land Rover.'

'And where did you dispose of the body?'

'Well, obviously, in the same place as I disposed of Phyllis's. And—' he smiled – 'where you will be very shortly joining them.' He looked across at his home-built travesty of a Lycian tomb. 'Very fitting, don't you think?'

And Carole understood why the stone blocks that floored

Travers Hughes-Swann's 'suntrap' had been so much less dusty and weed-covered than the rest of the garden. They had just been moved to accommodate Nita's body beneath them.

He had now unclipped the plastic catch which made the lanyard into a necklace and was wrapping the free ends around his strong thin hands. 'Now, obviously, it's going to be easier for me, Carole, if you don't struggle, but it won't make a lot of difference either way. I'm still going to kill you.'

Carole began to scream. She wondered why she hadn't thought of screaming before. But the nylon lanyard was so quickly round her neck, and so tightly round her neck that the screaming sound ended abruptly in a choke. She found her mind turning to her granddaughter Lily – and the brother or sister for Lily whom she would never meet.

Carole Seddon felt her consciousness draining away. She was only half-aware of a commotion at the gates of Brighton House, then a shout and the sound of a gun firing.

She didn't see Travers Hughes-Swann stagger, slacken his hold on the lanyard as his strength deserted him, and drop to the ground, dead.

THIRTY-TWO

There was no way the police could not be called this time. An ambulance was also summoned, but the paramedic who examined her announced that Carole did not need hospitalization. She would have a very sore throat for a few days, but the bruising would not take long to subside.

The police quickly established the basic facts, Barney having enough Turkish for them to understand each other. Erkan did not deny having shot Travers Hughes-Swann, and his action had been seen by Jude and Barney. There might have been a third witness, but Carole had been too near unconsciousness to be reliable.

The police said they would need to ask more questions, but,

given Carole's condition, they agreed that the three English could go next door to Morning Glory for the time being

In spite of her shock, Carole decided that she probably could manage a glass of wine – 'That nice one that tastes like Sauvignon Blanc,' she croaked. Soon the three of them were sitting round a poolside table. A rather odd assemblage – Carole recovering from near-strangulation, and Barney with his blood-soaked shoulder. Jude was the only one uninjured.

Carole should probably have gone to bed with some paracetamol, but she was far too intrigued by the missing bits of Jude's narrative. And the main thing she wanted to know was why Erkan, who when she last saw him had been issuing death threats against Barney, should suddenly be shooting Travers.

'He explained that,' said Jude, 'when he found us in the ghost town.'

'Sorry? In the ghost town?'

And Jude remembered that Carole had been asleep when she'd left Morning Glory. So she explained about the summons she had received from Barney, and how Travers had guided her to his hideaway.

'But he also told Erkan where Barney was, and Erkan immediately discharged himself from hospital and—'

'Yes, he told me that.'

'But Travers made a big mistake when he made that call to Erkan. He mentioned that Nita had been strangled with her lanyard. Now, in theory, the only people who knew how she died were you, Barney and Erkan. You all saw the body in the tomb. The reason Erkan came to find Barney in the ghost town was to check whether he'd told anyone about the lanyard. I could vouch for the fact that you wouldn't tell anyone, because you were keeping quiet about actually having *seen* the body. So, unless he'd actually murdered her, how did Travers know about the lanyard?'

Liking the logic she was hearing, Carole nodded (which was much less painful than speaking).

Jude went on, 'As soon as Erkan had established that Barney hadn't mentioned the lanyard to anyone, he announced that Travers must be the murderer and that he was going to shoot

him. We tried to persuade him not to, but he wouldn't listen
to us. Which, as it turned out, was a good thing for you.'

Gratefully, Carole smiled (another action less painful than
speaking).

Jude turned to Barney. 'So what do you reckon will happen
to Erkan? Prison sentences can be pretty harsh out here, can't
they?'

'Yes, but there would be a good few mitigating circumstances in his case. The fact that his shooting Erkan stopped
you being strangled, Carole, for one. He did it to save your
life. And if they can ever prove that Travers did kill Nita, the
case for Erkan's defence would be that much stronger.'

'Oh, but they will be able to,' croaked Carole, the importance
of what she had to say far outweighing the pain that saying
it might cause her. 'Nita's body is under the floor of Travers's
naff little suntrap. Along with that of his wife.'

Jude and Barney looked at her, open-mouthed.

And, despite her very sore throat, as an amateur sleuth
Carole Seddon did feel rather pleased with herself.

THIRTY-THREE

T he rest of Carole and Jude's stay in Kayaköy was
pleasantly uneventful which, given what had happened
in the first four days of the holiday, was probably just
as well. They got into a pleasant rhythm of doing some things
together and some separately. Sometimes they might be apart
at lunchtime, but they went out to eat together every evening.
They explored the varied cuisine on offer in some of the other
restaurants. They tried the more expensive options, the zhuzhed-
up boutique hotel Izela and the Lissiki Wine House. They had
excellent and reasonably priced meals at the Village Garden
(literally, someone's back garden) and the Villa Rhapsody
(known as Atilla's after its ebullient owner).

But more often than not they ended up eating in the casual
welcoming atmosphere of Antik. And Jude failed regularly to

stop having a large wonderfully cold beer before she moved on to the wine.

At the beginning of their second week they even went together to the archaeological site of Tlos to experience more of the Lycian culture. They climbed up the high rock, marvelling at the ingenuity and mindset of a civilization that would choose to build tombs in such inaccessible places.

But Carole still didn't get the 'TLOS PROPERTY' joke.

One day they went to the fabulous sandy beach at Patara, but before they did anything else Carole insisted they should visit the ruined city, recently and very impressively excavated. After that they rented loungers. Jude stripped down to her bikini and sploshed about in the bracingly large waves, while Carole kept her trousers on and, sitting awkwardly on the edge of her lounger, tried to concentrate on one of her *Times* crosswords. Jude would have been happy to stay on the beach till it got dark, but aware of her friend's lack of ease, agreed to leave about two. They had an excellent late lunch in a restaurant called Ayak in a nearby village, then returned to Morning Glory to laze by the pool.

As the days went by, Carole's throat got less sore and, having gone through the spectrum from purple to yellow, her bruises slowly faded.

One morning they were visited at Morning Glory by the police – two very correct young officers who spoke excellent English. Both women made statements about the events of the Thursday evening. The policemen took their contact details but said there would be no need for them to change their travel arrangements. They could return to England the following Monday as planned.

They didn't see Barney Willingdon again while they were out in Turkey. As soon as Henry was reunited with her husband, she had booked them on the first flight back to England, where she very soon forced him to consult a specialist in erectile dysfunction. It is to be hoped, given the amount of trouble it had caused to so many people, that his problem was sorted out. Maybe Viagra worked its magic, but Carole and Jude never found out because the Willingdons didn't contact them again after they'd returned to Fethering.

On the Wednesday of their second week, as an indication of how much she was entering into the holiday spirit, Carole Seddon did two things she had sworn she never would. She bought a trashy novel (there were plenty of books in English available in Fethiye).

And, even more daringly, she bought a plain black bikini.

Then she spent a lot of the remainder of their time at Morning Glory reading the one and wearing the other, lying at the poolside with Jude a few loungers away. And when she'd finished – and, it had to be said, rather enjoyed – her Danielle Steel, she started reading *Fifty Shades of Grey* (only, of course, to see what all the fuss was about).

She'd long ago stopped wearing her money belt. She no longer even noticed the *muezzin*'s daily calls to prayer. As the days went by there seemed to be less and less urgency to go and see any more archaeological sites.

And Carole Seddon almost – dare it be said? – relaxed.

When, on the Monday morning, the pre-booked taxi arrived to take them to Dalaman Airport, Morning Glory was living up to its name, the frontage of the villa a splendid display of blue.

The weather was good when they got back to England, late that afternoon. Even though they had return railway tickets, Carole did not demur when Jude said they should get a cab from Gatwick to Fethering.

They parted on the pavement between their two houses. Jude went back to Woodside Cottage and began to check through the list of messages on her answering machine. She dealt with most of her client work on the landline, only allowing a favoured few her mobile number or email address. If she didn't protect herself in that way, she knew that she'd get no peace with constant day and night 'emergency' calls from her frequently paranoid clientele.

The first thing Carole did on her return to High Tor was to unpack (she had fixed to pick up Gulliver the following morning). She felt a slight pang as she folded away the black bikini and the beige cotton shorts, but then pulled herself together. There were things one might do in Kayaköy that one wouldn't dream of doing in Fethering. So Carole Seddon's legs were removed from public view for at least another decade.

As soon as she had finished unpacking and put on a load of washing, she rang through to Fulham.

Gaby sounded extremely perky when she answered the phone. In the background, Lily could be heard chattering away nineteen to the dozen.

'Just checking in.'

'Oh yes?'

'To say I'm safely back from Turkey.'

'Ah.' Gaby had clearly forgotten her mother-in-law had been away, but covered the lapse very quickly. 'Oh, great. Did you have a good time?'

'Very good, thank you,' said Carole, surprising herself actually to be telling the truth. 'And how have you been?'

'Fine.'

'I meant about the pregnancy.'

'That's fine too. Still pregnant, everything where it should be.'

'No more sickness?'

'No, thank the Lord.'

'And Stephen's in good form?'

'Oh, as ever. You know Stephen.'

'Yes,' said Carole, though she sometimes wondered whether she actually did. 'Any other news?'

'Not really.'

Carole still wasn't sure whether the teddy bear with Union Jack shorts was a suitable present for her granddaughter, or whether it was too common, but she made the decision quickly and said, 'I did buy a little something for Lily.'

'Oh, she'll be delighted.'

'And I thought I could give it to her when I next see you.'

'Great.'

'Which I hope will be very soon.' And it was a measure of how much the holiday had done for her confidence that Carole then went on to ask, 'I wonder, are you around this coming weekend? If you are, I could come up on Sunday.'

It was the first time she had ever invited herself to Fulham. Normally, she waited until an invitation had been issued. But the relaxed way in which Gaby said that would be great and they'd love to see her made Carole feel that her previous inhibitions had been unnecessary. And that brought rather a warm glow to her.

Then Gaby called out to ask if Lily would like to speak to Granny, and Carole got a very full and detailed account of everything that was happening in her granddaughter's three-year-old life.

After the call had ended, Carole felt rather at a loose end. She still wasn't out of holiday mood, and it seemed like the time to go out to one of Kayaköy's bars for a drink.

So she rang Jude and suggested they pay a visit to the Crown and Anchor.

'Blimey, you never got that tan in England,' said Ted Crisp as they entered the bar.

'No, it's from Turkey,' said Carole Seddon, the relaxed cosmopolitan traveller.

'Oh,' said Ted. 'Yes, of course, you told me you were going. Incidentally, do you know what's the best way to serve Turkey?'

'We know that one,' said Jude. 'You've asked us before.'

'Have I?' said Ted, looking a little disturbed. Though his jokes were almost always dreadful, he prided himself on not telling them more than once to the same person. 'What's the answer then?'

'Join the Turkish army,' said Jude.

'Oh damn, you did know it.' Ted reached down to the wine fridge. 'Two large Chilean Chardonnays, is it?'

'No,' said Carole boldly. 'Could you make it two large Sauvignon Blancs?'

'Bloody hell,' said Ted Crisp.

And as the two women sat down at the bar to talk about their holiday in Turkey, Carole realized that, the whole time she'd been there, she hadn't taken a single Imodium.